LOVE TRIANGLE

All her life, Sophie's known the Cassell brothers — after all they are the boys next door . . . But suddenly Sophie's life has become very, very complicated. Because she's just fallen madly, deeply in love with Adrian Cassell. And while Adrian barely knows she exists, Ian Cassell seems to have fallen for her . . . Can Sophie persuade Ade she's the woman of his dreams, without hurting Ian? Or are they stuck in love's eternal triangle? When you fall for the boy next door, life's never easy. But Sophie's just about to learn how bad it can get . . .

Point R♥mance

LOVE TRIANGLE

Lorna Read

Complete and Unabridged

spectrum
LARGE PRINT

First published in Great Britain in 1996 by
Scholastic Children's Books
London

First Large Print Edition
published 2000
by arrangement with
Scholastic Children's Books
London

British Library CIP Data

Read, Lorna
    Love triangle.—Large print ed.—
    (Point romance)—Spectrum imprint
    1. Love stories
    2. Children's stories
    3. Large type books
    I. Title
    823.9'14 [J]

    ISBN 0–7089–9506–3

Published by
F. A. Thorpe (Publishing)
Anstey, Leicestershire

Set by Words & Graphics Ltd.
Anstey, Leicestershire
Printed and bound in Great Britain by
T. J. International Ltd., Padstow, Cornwall

This book is printed on acid-free paper

1

He was tall, he was lean, his jeans were torn and faded, but his T-shirt was unbelievably clean and white. As he bent over the bonnet of his car, the white cotton pulled upwards, exposing a length of back that was tanned a light golden-brown by the Spring sun. Sophie sucked her breath in through clenched teeth and narrowed her eyes as she watched him. 'Adrian Cassell, you are a dream!' she said out loud.

He had always loved cars and had taken his driving test as soon as he could. Sophie could remember how overjoyed he was when he came rushing back with the good news. His father had opened a bottle of wine and they had all wished him an accident-free future on the roads. He bought an old car straight away, with money he had saved. Since then he'd owned a succession of old bangers which he had spent all his spare time restoring, polishing up and re-selling. The green Austin was the latest in the line.

He finished inspecting the engine, stood up, turned round and stretched. Sophie tried willing him to look up and see her standing at her bedroom window. But just as he appeared about to look her way, she ducked down, hurling herself into a crouching position on her bedside rug. She had decided that she most definitely *didn't* want him to see her after all. It would be awkward ... embarrassing ... *impossible*, if he discovered the way her feelings about him had changed.

So she sat down heavily on the edge of her bed and sighed, thinking if only life could go back to being as simple as it had been just a few weeks ago, before she had gone and done the most stupid thing any girl could ever do — fallen in love with, of all people, the boy next door. And right in the middle of revising for her exams, too! What absolutely terrible timing. How could she possibly swot when all she wanted to do was think about Adrian?

There were, actually, two boys next door. But Ian, Adrian's younger brother, although great company and a real laugh, didn't count at all in the romance stakes. If there had been a Eurovision Boy Contest, Ian would have scored *nul points*. Not because he was gruesome-looking or anything, but because he was . . . well, sort of nothingy, really. Reddish-brown hair, brown eyes, medium build, like so many other boys. Nothing special. Just dead average.

Adrian, though, was perfect. He was dark-haired and handsome, in a rock-star sort of way, and had recently celebrated his nineteenth birthday. He wasn't going out with anybody as far as she knew; at least, she hadn't seen him bring a girl home. Another perfect thing about him was that he was taller than she was. Sophie had grown three inches between the ages of thirteen and sixteen and was now five-feet-eight — taller than that in her favourite shoes. Ian was only about her height. He'd have to reach up to kiss her if she had her black shoes on.

Not that she ever fantasized about kissing Ian! Ade was another matter entirely. His lips . . . mmm! They were thin and mean-looking. A kiss from him would be firm and dry and purposeful. He would sweep her against him in a tight embrace and his warm, dry mouth would press firm, persuasive kisses against hers and . . .

From here, her imaginings usually led to a romantic proposal, then a dreamy white wedding followed by the two of them moving into a country cottage, like the ones her family usually rented in Devon or Wales for a fortnight in the summer.

Sophie and Adrian Cassell, with the emphasis on the 'ell'; Sophie Cassell sounded really good, like an actress's name. Much better than boring Thompson! It was a French name, Tara Cassell had explained.

The Cassells had moved next door to the Thompsons more than a dozen years ago, so the five children — Tara, Ian and Adrian, and Sophie and her older brother Richard — had practically grown up together. For as long as Sophie could remember, they had been like one big, happy, extended family. They had shared heartaches and holidays, bicycles and barbecues, school notes and sports equipment. Tara, a few months younger than Sophie, was her oldest friend. Though each had made new friends in their respective classes at school, they were still like sisters to one another. And Ian and Ade had always been like two extra brothers.

So when had things changed?

It was hard to pin-point the exact moment when the teasing, rough-and-tumble, scabby-kneed, soccer-playing Ade had ceased to be like a brother and had turned into Adrian the cool dresser, witty talker and object of intense and unrequited desire. He might have been like that for months, but Sophie had only noticed three weeks ago . . .

* * *

The two families had joined forces on a day out, as they often did. Their expeditions were often connected to school-work. As Ian had to write a project on castles, it was decided that they should go to Framlingham in Suffolk, where there was a castle dating back to the 1100s, built on the site of an earlier Anglo-Saxon one.

Sophie loved old places. They gave her the creeps, in a thrilling sort of way. She loved the cold, old atmosphere of them, loved placing her hands on old stone and wishing she could be whisked back in time.

The approach to Framlingham Castle was over a walkway across a ditch. Ahead, the immense walls, eight feet thick and with a walkway right along the top, rose forty feet into the air. Thirteen rectangular towers were spaced along the walls, each tower rising another twenty feet into the stormy sky. Some of the towers were mere lumps of stone but others retained much of their original stonework, complete with slits for shooting arrows through.

Ian and Richard rushed on ahead to see who could get up the hill to the castle the quickest. Tara had stomach-ache and was lagging behind with the two mothers. The dads were poring over an Ordnance Survey map of the area. Earlier in the day there had been a sudden heavy shower and the sky had been dark with billowing nimbus clouds. Now the clouds were rolling up like the edge of a sardine can, exposing a brilliant strip of oily yellow sky. Sophie raised her eyes to admire the dramatic spectacle and suddenly spotted Adrian standing on a chunk of broken battlement, silhouetted against the sky, his head haloed by a shaft of sunlight that was just breaking free of the cloud.

Her breath caught in her throat. This wasn't Ade her next door neighbour any more. She had been swept backwards in time and this breathtakingly handsome young man, standing in such a dramatic pose, was the lord of the castle, about to lead his troops into battle to defend his lands. This was not a twentieth-century leather jacket that he wore, but a heavy, swirling cloak made of the finest deer hide, encrusted with jewels and embroidery. The strap over his shoulder bore the weight of a sword, not a camera, while the object in his hand was not a guide-book but an embossed shield.

She took a couple of steps back and narrowed her eyes, her imagination adding the final touches to her historical fantasy. Adrian turned his head slowly, scanning the panorama around him. As he did so, there was a wild *chak-chak* sound and a pair of jackdaws flew out of a crevice in the tumbled stones. Seconds later, the cause of the disturbance was revealed as Ian appeared with a branch, pretending it was a crossbow which he was firing from the battlements.

Cursing to herself, she dragged her eyes away from the vision which was now on the move, striding along the ridge towards a knot of people clustered around a guide, giving a potted history of the castle to a group of tourists. Sophie could just hear his voice, carried on the wind: 'The Great Hall no longer exists, having been incorporated into the poorhouse, built in the early seventeenth century by Pembroke College, Cambridge, who had bought the site . . . '

Someone called her name. She turned to see Tara, obviously feeling better, running towards her and waving. She smiled and went to meet her friend. Everyone gathered together and the two families spread plastic sheets in the shelter of a wall and unwrapped their sandwiches.

As she ate, Sophie found herself continually glancing at Ade and thinking how his shortened name didn't really suit him now that he was no longer a scruffy boy like the other two. How had she missed him growing up? Why had it taken until today to discover that he had stopped giggling and looning around with Richard and Ian, and had grown dignified; distant, somehow? Where had that dignity come from? And when had he developed those haunting cheek-bones and that look in his eyes, as if he was gazing to a far horizon, like the lord of the castle whom she had imagined him to be?

Richard prodded her, saying, 'Oi, Sis, pass us one of those chicken thingummies, will you?'

Sophie had passed the plastic container of tandoori chicken legs without uttering a word. She was lost in thought and was only dragged back to the present when a sudden gust of wind caught her empty lemonade can and sent it rolling down the hillside.

She sprang to her feet, preparing to dash after it, but Adrian was too quick for her. His long legs quickly covered the distance and retrieved the can from its resting place against a bush. He came back and pressed it firmly down into the plastic bag where they were putting their litter. Seeing Sophie watching him, he smiled.

Adrian Cassell had smiled at Sophie Thompson at least a million times in the last twelve years, but this was the first time she had not only seen his smile but felt it, too. His smile broke over her like a wave over a rock, only she was much softer than a rock and far less able to withstand the force of it. She felt as if she were reeling backwards. She felt her face grow hot and she looked down at her paper plate, feeling a complete idiot and hoping nobody was noticing her confusion.

People were speaking to her: her father, asking if she'd like a cheese and Marmite sandwich; Richard, the nature freak, talking knowledgeably about jackdaws; Tara, saying something about a swimming gala; and it was all turning into a blathering babble inside her brain.

She sneaked a glance at Adrian from under her lashes and — thrill! horror! — he was looking at her. He smiled again, and once more she felt the shockwave hit her and she almost choked on a smoky bacon crisp.

For the rest of that day she had felt stiff and tense and acutely self-conscious. Her hand constantly strayed to her hair, tidying it, and her eyes continually scanned as much as she could see of herself to make sure nothing embarrassing had occurred, such as mud splashes on her socks or trainers, or moss from the rock she had leaned against getting caught in her hair. Her hair was so thick and curly that things were always getting tangled in it. She had curls which shot out of her scalp like corkscrews. The light brown mass was like a lion's mane and challenged the teeth of every comb she introduced to it, with her curls always winning the battle.

She was glad when Tara agreed to travel home on the back seat of the Thompson's car, next to her, with the remaining Cassells occupying the other car. Two and a half hours' close proximity to Adrian would have done her no good whatsoever.

Somehow, she managed to reply to Tara's chatter although her mind was elsewhere, full of the incredible discovery she had made. Fancy, all these years she had been living next door to the boy she was destined to fall in love with. She would live happily with him for the rest of her life. Who would ever have guessed it? It happened in movies and love stories, of course, but when it did, you knew it was only a story and too convenient to be true. Yet now the unbelievable really had happened. She had found true love right where she least expected to find it — on her very own doorstep!

2

From the moment she returned home, Sophie's life was turned upside-down. Some people joke about having 'x-ray eyes', but Sophie thought she was developing 'x-ray ears' because every sound, every squeak, from the house next door seemed magnified, and a subject for speculation. Was that Adrian opening a door? Was that faint music a CD he was listening to? There was next door's phone ringing: was it a girl asking for Adrian? He hung around a lot with her brother Richard, and he had enough girls after him. But she was sure she would know if either of them had a regular girlfriend.

The morning after she had watched Adrian tinkering with his car, Sophie was walking along Kendal Street on her way to school. Suddenly, she spotted a familiar figure ahead of her, wearing a sea-green shirt and beige chinos. As it was the very same person who had caused her to lie awake for a long time the night before, she slowed down. She didn't want to catch him up because she didn't have a clue what to say to him, so she stood and watched him. He'd gelled his hair and in the May sunshine it looked full of gleamy lights, like starling's wings.

They were near the parade of local shops. Adrian walked into the newsagent's and Sophie quickened her pace, intending to be round the corner of the street by the time he emerged. But he must have got served straight away because he came out clutching a magazine just as Sophie drew level with the door.

'Hi-ya, Sophe!' he greeted her.

'Hello, Adrian,' she replied.

'*Adrian?*' he asked. 'What's wrong with Ade? You're looking very serious this morning. Anything wrong?'

Oh, that look! she thought. He looked really concerned, really interested. In her? Or only in her supposed problem? She prayed it was her.

'Nothing, really,' she replied. 'It just seems a real waste of a lovely day to have to be shut up in a classroom till four.'

'Yeah, I used to feel like that, too,' he said, matching his steps to hers as they walked along side-by-side. 'But now I've

13

left, I miss it. Miss learning things. Miss the lads.'

He had left school at sixteen and had done a course in catering and hotel management, but hadn't been able to find a job yet. She felt sorry for him and asked the ritual question, the one she asked regularly at least once a week.

'Any interviews on the horizon?'

His face brightened. 'Yes, as a matter of fact. I've got one this afternoon. At the new car showroom in Fairfax Road.'

'You mean that place next to the hairdresser's? But I've looked in the window and seen those cars. They cost upwards of twelve thousand pounds!'

Sophie's eyes widened in amazement and she stopped walking. 'Don't you need special training for that?'

'They want some smart lads to train up.'

'Maybe you'll get a discount on a limo.'

They stood looking at each other for a moment that felt more awkward by the micro-second. Then Sophie glanced at her watch. 'Oh, heavens, I'm really late! I've got to run. Good luck this afternoon!' She gave him a thumbs-up sign and raced down to the crossing while the lights were still in her favour. She didn't stop running until she was on the other side of the main road, heading for the school gates. Then she slowed, and turned, and looked, but he had vanished, swallowed up by the morning crowds.

⭐ ⭐ ⭐

It was Richard, not Adrian, who brought her the news that evening.

'Oh, guess what?' he said casually, stirring the cup of hot chocolate he had just made for himself. 'Ade's got a job as a trainee manager at that new car place. Lucky so-and-so. Do you know how much he'll be earning while he's still training?'

He mentioned a sum which made Sophie exclaim, 'Wow!'

'*And* he gets commission on top of that if he sells anything. It's going to be years before I earn anything like that amount,' Richard said, enviously. He was in his final year at school and was hoping to go to university in the autumn to do an engineering course. 'It'll improve his pulling power no end,' he added, even more enviously.

'What do you mean?' Sophie's mind was

still on cars and the thought of her brother as a student.

'With the girls, thicko. Pulling. As in 'getting off with'. Snogging. Do I make myself clear?'

'Who'd want to snog you?' Sophie retorted, poking her tongue out at her brother, whose fair curls looked in dire need of a comb. Yet her heart was thumping and she didn't know why.

But once Richard had carried his drink upstairs to his room, and she was left staring at the pinkish-brown blobs of spilled chocolate on the white work-top, she realized it was fear that was making her feel so uncomfortable. Fear that some other girl would catch Adrian's eye and start going out with him before s Sophie, could make him see her as person, an attractive female one at that, rather than the honorary sister, the taken-for-granted girl next door.

★ ★ ★

It was Saturday again, at last, and as Sophie wheeled her bicycle up the side of the house, she was hoping against hope that Adrian would be out at the front. A bright, expectant grin was already forming on her face and she had carefully done her hair, catching back some of her wild tangle of curls in a red band on top of her head. She had also put some make-up on, the merest touch; mascara and a dab of gloss shadow to make her green eyes sparkle, and the faintest tinge of lipstick.

She was wearing cut-off denims and a red T-shirt, red socks and trainers which she had spent twenty minutes cleaning so that they were an immaculate white. Normally, she was quite careless about her clothes, unless it was a special occasion. But lately, every minute of every day seemed like a special occasion, because she had to be constantly ready in case she bumped into Ade.

Ade . . . Adrian. She'd called him Ade for years but she couldn't help feeling that his full name suited him best now. It was definitely suaver. 'Ade' sounded better suited to a more casual, scruffy bloke, but 'Adrian' was definitely the right name for the manager of a luxury car showroom. She could just picture him in a smart suit, ushering rich people into shiny limousines and taking them out for a test drive.

Just for the teeniest moment, she

pictured herself and Adrian sitting in the back of a classic open-top Rolls Royce, he in a dark suit and she in a billowy white dress and veil, being showered with confetti. Then she shook her head and dismissed this most forbidden of all fantasies. Her friends would think her really soppy if she confessed to ideas about white weddings. They were all into having careers and not settling down until they had achieved something, whereas she felt love should always come first. Anyone could work, but not everyone could find perfect love, and when you *did* find it, you had to grab it and hang on to it and make sure you didn't lose it.

It would be super having Tara as a sister-in-law ... Oh, there she was, off again!

There was no sign of Adrian, which was a bitter blow. She had to take her books and her mother's back to the library before lunch, so she had to get going. Where could Adrian be?

As she was standing, hand poised on the handlebars, staring at the Cassells' house, the front door opened and Sophie's heart missed a beat. But the smiling male that greeted her was Ian, not Ade.

'Hi! If you're going to the library, I'll come with you,' he said. 'Just let me get my bike.'

Oh, no! thought Sophie crossly. The last thing she wanted was for Adrian to see her going off somewhere with his little brother. Then she told herself off for being stupid. He wouldn't think anything of it, because various combinations of Thompsons and Cassells were always going off and doing things together, and always had done.

'Oh, OK then,' she said. 'But be quick. I've got to be back here by one.'

As Ian disappeared round the corner, Sophie heaved a deep sigh. Why was it that other girls did things with their boyfriends on Saturdays and she was stuck with cycling to the library with Ian from next door? What was wrong with her, she wondered. Nobody had asked her out for ages. Though it could be something to do with exams. Everyone she knew had their heads buried in their books. By rights, with her GCSEs coming up, she should be swotting right now. But, as she'd said to her mum, she had to get some fresh air sometime. And anyway, as she hadn't got a boyfriend, she could

19

swot every night of the week.

She hadn't been out with anyone since Brian Hooper, last November. That's if you could call Brian Hooper a boyfriend. Although they'd gone out for two months, he'd only held her hand and never even made a move to kiss her. Tara and she had often giggled about it, inventing reasons for his reluctance to kiss, such as dreadful breath, or false teeth.

Sophie had given him the elbow because she was just plain bored. She hadn't really been interested in him. She'd never been even vaguely in love with anybody, before Adrian. And now it had hit her full blast, an unending ache inside her midriff region and a yearning, choking sensation in her throat which made her feel constantly on the brink of tears. Oh, he was so wonderful . . . he was everything. Surely one day he would suddenly start feeling the same way about her? Or was he feeling it already and was just too shy to tell her? Too worried about changing the relationship that had existed between them for so long?

Her deep thoughts had to come to an end because Ian plus bike appeared. 'Beat you to the end of the road!' he yelled.

Oh, what a kid he still was, reflected Sophie, watching him tear off in a cloud of dust and small pebbles. She mounted her bike and rode after him at a leisurely pace. By the time she reached the end of Pevensey Crescent, Ian had leant his bike against a tree and was poised with one foot still on the pedal, looking perplexed.

'It was a race,' he said accusingly.

'I know,' responded Sophie, airily.

'So why didn't you race me?'

'I didn't want to.'

'Why not?' he demanded.

She noticed that his hair looked the exact colour of the copper beech tree he stood beneath. An odd shade of purple.

'I . . . I just didn't feel like it,' she said.

Ian shrugged and a faint flush tinged his cheeks. For a second, he looked very like Adrian, and Sophie felt confused.

'Because it's a hot day. I felt like taking things easy,' she babbled, then added crossly, 'Oh, come on, let's get to the library.' It was herself she was cross with, not Ian. He hadn't done anything — except not be Adrian.

Once at the library, though, they had a laugh. The library assistant who checked in their returned books had a piece of lettuce stuck to her chin. Sophie and Ian exchanged glances and suppressed their laughter so much that once they'd got through the barrier into the library itself, they collapsed against a filing cabinet, gasping and snorting and trying not to disturb everybody else.

Libraries are places of such forced silence that they make you feel more like laughing than ever. In the end, they gave up trying to choose books and made a bolt for the sunshine outside, where they collapsed against a wall, doubled up and holding their stomachs.

Then suddenly, all the laughter drained away from Sophie. Adrian was walking past. No, not walking, exactly. 'Sauntering' would have described it better. He was in no hurry, for the simple reason that he was laughing and chatting to somebody. A girl. Sophie's teeth clenched so hard that her head hurt. How *dare* this unknown girl be polluting the air-space next to Adrian? How dare she have waist-length honey-blonde hair, all shiny and straight and beautifully trimmed, and legs as long and willowy as a giraffe's?

And as knobbly, Sophie observed ungenerously. She was aware of Ian's unwanted presence by her side. He was ominously silent. She turned away from the sight that was tormenting her, to look at Ian, and caught him looking at her. But as fast as her eyes spotted his look, his eyes slid away and over into the distance somewhere. He didn't speak and, with another jolt of insight, she knew that *he* knew.

Oh, heavens, she thought. He's guessed I'm crazy about his brother. *Now* what's going to happen? Can I trust him?

Ian didn't say anything, just started unlocking his bike rather clangingly. She felt annoyed. She didn't want him there. She wanted to be alone to lick her wounds and plan what to do next.

Ian was wheeling his bike across the pavement to the road. He was leaving her.

'Got to go see a friend,' he muttered. 'See you.' And he was off, pedalling a rather wavery route along the inside of a double-decker bus.

Meanwhile, Adrian and the enemy had turned into the 'Cosmos Café'.

I must be a masochist, Sophie thought grimly as she wheeled her bike past the café's main window. There they were, settling themselves at a table against the wall. They hadn't seen her. Adrian was talking animatedly and the girl was gazing avidly at him, mopping up every word.

I hope you spill your coffee all down that lily-white blouse of yours, Sophie willed viciously, kicking her bike and making the pedals spin. Then she thought *poor bike*, and stroked its saddle, feeling tears well up in her eyes. It wasn't the bike's fault that Adrian was so obtuse. He obviously needed time; time to realize Sophie-next-door was the most wonderful, desirable, beautiful girl in the whole of Britain; time to figure out that he was in love with her and females like Ms Giraffe Legs were like fallen petals floating on a lake. Lovely, but transient, soon to disappear.

And with that poetic thought, she pedalled for home.

3

Richard was tweaking his blond hair in front of the hall mirror, trying to make his moussed curls lie flat, when Sophie sneaked up on him that evening.

'So where's big brother going tonight, looking so spruced-up, eh?' she teased. 'Shouldn't you be staying in and swotting, like me?'

She was very fond of Richard, even if he did tease her rather a lot. He was built like a rugby player, with broad shoulders and a powerful frame. Girls found him gorgeous. Sophie was always being asked to help arrange dates between besotted girls and her brother. Richard was a kind, caring, sensible sort of boy. His popularity didn't seem to have gone to his head. He was easy-going and always good for a laugh. But, although he often went out in a crowd, he rarely took a girl out on her own for a date, and never more than once.

When Sophie asked why, he explained that he wasn't ready to get serious, and he didn't want to give anyone the wrong idea.

If he went out with someone more than once, they might read more into it than he intended. He didn't want a heavy involvement as he was applying for university, and didn't know where he'd end up.

'I'm going out for a drink with Ade,' he said.

Sophie's heart almost stopped beating. Oh, how unfair that Adrian should be sharing his time with Richard, not her! What were they up to? She couldn't believe that a drink was all these two good-looking guys had planned. Did they have a couple of girls lined up? That leggy blonde, plus a friend of hers for Richard? How could she find out?

'Where are you going?' she asked.

'Just out,' he replied, grinning infuriatingly. 'Why do you want to know?'

He was staring curiously at her and Sophie could feel the heat tingling in her face. 'I don't, really. I was just making polite conversation,' she said, turning away. She felt wild with jealousy. Why couldn't he invite her along, too? But of course he couldn't, if Adrian was meeting that blonde!

She was already half-way up the stairs to

her room, where her text-books awaited her, when Richard called up after her. 'We're only going to 'The Castle' for a game of pool. You wouldn't have wanted to come, anyway.'

'You're right!' she shouted down to him. 'I wouldn't be seen dead in that smoky old grot-hole.' *And neither would the blonde*, she thought triumphantly.

A ring of the doorbell signified Adrian's arrival, at which Sophie hastily dived into her room, not wanting him to see her dressed in her tattiest jeans and with her hair in a mess. With her bedroom door open a crack, she could hear the boys' voices rising up the stairs, but though she strained her ears, she couldn't catch what they were saying. Then there was the sound of the front door slamming and then the twin bangs of the car doors. Sophie raced to the window in time to see them driving away. Oh, how her heart ached. Why couldn't she be sitting in the passenger seat next to Adrian, just the two of them? To work! she told herself firmly, opening her copy of *Romeo and Juliet*. Since falling in love with Adrian, she had found it extremely easy to learn certain passages, such as:

My bounty is as boundless as the sea,
My love as deep; the more I give to
   thee,
The more I have, for both are infinite.

But would she be able to use the passages she knew so well by heart in examination answers? And the exam was on Monday! *Oh, Romeo . . . oh, Adrian!* she sighed.

Just before eleven, Sophie's mother popped her head round the door and said she was going to bed. Jim Thompson, Sophie's father, was away on business and not due back till Wednesday. Brenda Thompson said it was wonderful to be able to stretch out and have the whole bed to herself instead of having to compete for space with a sixteen-stone male.

Sophie couldn't imagine herself ever having the same problem. She could never fancy anyone as big and broad as her dad. She liked slim, sleek guys . . . like Adrian. What *was* he up to tonight? She closed her books and got into bed. But she couldn't sleep. It got to midnight and Richard still wasn't back, so she got up and watched a ghost movie till one-thirty. Richard and Adrian still weren't back. Where on earth were they? In the end, she just had to go to bed without knowing.

* * *

Richard came down late to breakfast next day, and it was a great relief to Sophie to see him. He looked dreadful and said he had a hangover. When Sophie tried to question him, he grunted and turned away and pretended to be reading a post-card that had arrived for him from his American pen-friend, but Sophie knew he wasn't really reading it as he was holding it upside-down.

After a spell of glorious weather, the sky was looking overcast and heavy with rain. Richard toyed with a piece of toast, let it grow cold and hard, then announced that he needed some fresh air and disappeared into the garden.

She went back into her own room and rapped smartly on the wall. There was an answering knock from Tara. They used their code to arrange that Tara should call round to see Sophie in fifteen minutes.

Tara's gleaming red-gold hair was lying in a plait over one shoulder, secured with a purple band. Instead of a T-shirt, she was sporting a teddy-bear-patterned top which was clearly the upper part of her pyjamas, worn over dark blue leggings. But for all her sloppy, first-thing-in-the-morning attire, her eyes were bright and sparkly and her face bore a bright smile.

'I had a great night last night!' she said.

'I didn't,' Sophie countered gloomily.

'What happened to you, then?'

'Oh, a few theorems just fell into place. I suddenly understood the meaning of life, the universe and everything.'

'Wish *I* did,' Sophie groaned.

'But you're not taking Physics and Chemistry,' Tara pointed out.

'I know. But I'd still like to understand what makes everything tick. You know. What makes it rain one day and be sunny the next. What makes one boy fancy you and another boy be totally indifferent, even — ' Sophie felt her body grow tense with longing — 'even when you're so madly in love with him that it should be obvious to the whole world.'

Tara looked at her with interest. 'Who are you in love with, then?' she asked.

'Um, no one, it was just a figure of speech,' Sophie lied.

Tara's lips screwed up in a 'don't believe you' expression.

'It's true!' Sophie protested. 'There is no boy in the whole wide world with whom I'm even slightly in love.' She had to lie. How could she possibly tell Tara it was her older brother? She would never hear the end of it!

'Nor me,' Tara echoed. 'Well, maybe . . . ' she started to add, but Sophie had switched off. She had a burning question on her mind, one that could no longer wait for an answer.

She tried to make her voice sound casual, as if she wasn't really interested in the reply. But she was, she was burning to know. 'Richard must have got in really late last night. He was looking shattered at breakfast. Any idea what time Ade got back?'

'I haven't a clue,' Tara said. 'I was dead tired after revising and was out cold.'

Sophie held her breath.

'Who cares, anyway?' continued Tara, oblivious to Sophie's distress. 'He's nineteen, he's a grown man. He can do what he likes. He doesn't have to be in by midnight.'

'I suppose not,' said Sophie mechanically. 'Same with Richard. Though Mum and Dad do prefer it if he tells them whether he's going to be in or out, then they can lock the doors.'

'So Richard came back last night, then?' Tara asked.

'Yes,' Sophie confirmed. 'I told you. I saw him at breakfast.' If her wits had been working normally, she might have thought Tara's question about Richard a bit odd and her tone rather over-curious. But she was too obsessed about Adrian's whereabouts to think normally.

'I haven't seen Ade today,' said Tara. Sophie held her breath. 'He's probably still snoring if he didn't get back till the early hours. Oh, well, as long as he had fun!'

Tara shot Sophie a meaningful look that was almost a wink. Sophie hated the idea of Adrian 'having fun'. She didn't want to think about him wasting himself on other girls when he should be with her, the girl he'd grown up with, the only right one for him!

Tara interrupted Sophie's dark thoughts by asking, 'Do you think Richard will let us play *Monkey Island* on his computer?' *Monkey Island* was a game about pirates and buried treasure which they both enjoyed.

32

'I'm sure he will, but I'd better go and ask him,' Sophie said.

She guessed that Richard had gone to the garden shed, where he kept the pieces of motorbike he was forever hoping to build into one that actually worked. Sophie went out there and as she approached the shed, she heard two male voices coming from it. It must be Ian, she thought. Ian was keen on motorbikes and often lent Richard a hand.

She pushed open the door — to find herself so close to Adrian that their faces were almost touching. Wobbly with shock, she took a step back and tried to act as if everything was perfectly normal.

I mustn't blush . . . please don't let me blush! she prayed.

'Oh, hello,' she said, trying to sound casually friendly. 'Anyone like a coffee? And Richard, do you mind if Tara and I play *Monkey Island* on your computer?'

'Yes, please. And yes, of course you can. You know how to switch it on?'

Sophie nodded vaguely, in a daze of bliss.

'Yes, please, two sugars,' echoed Adrian. Oh, his voice was so wonderful, a bit husky and so sexy. 'Brown sugar, if you've got it,' he added.

She wanted to say, 'You shouldn't be having sugar, you'll get fat,' but she didn't want him to think she was growing into a nagging woman, so she remained quiet, yet directed an appraising look at his neat waistline. Even in filthy old clothes he managed to look good enough to eat. His black jeans had darker patches on them which must be oil. His red-and-navy check cotton shirt was hanging loose and was similarly splodged, and both boys' hands were filthy.

Cleaning rags and pieces of metal littered the floor. Sophie was scared to move in case she kicked anything and got told off, so she left, feeling a lightness in her step that hadn't been there before. Adrian *had* come back last night. He'd be in bed recovering now if he hadn't. He definitely wouldn't be looking and sounding so wide awake. She'd been given a reprieve, and now it was entirely up to her to woo him and win him!

4

If only I knew what he really thought about me, Sophie agonized as she made the coffee. But, short of coming right out and asking him, how could she find out? She couldn't confide in Richard. He'd laugh his head off and treat it as a big joke. He still saw her as his kid sister. He'd think it was just a crush and he might say something to Adrian. Much as she loved him, she couldn't trust him. Not with a secret as great as this.

Tara or Ian might know something. They might have picked up on something Adrian had said, or noticed him looking at her in a certain way. She couldn't possibly ask Ian, though. After that supremely embarrassing incident at the library when he'd caught her staring at Adrian with that certain look in her eye, she'd tried to keep as far away from him as possible.

As for Tara . . . well, she didn't feel quite ready to tell her best friend that she was in love with her brother. It might alter something in their friendship, throw it out of kilter, somehow; Tara might feel jealous and think Sophie only wanted to come round to see Adrian, not her. It was too awkward, somehow. She'd just have to do her own detective work. But how?

Having made the coffee, she went upstairs to tell Tara the good news about the game and ask her to go into Richard's room and turn on his computer. Once Tara had gone across the landing, Sophie swiftly twisted a scarlet-coloured velvet band into her hair, hauling some of the thick, hay-coloured mass up on top and off her face. She rummaged among the make-up lying in her dressing-table drawer, took out a plastic palette and dabbed on a faint gleam of coppery-coloured eye-shadow. A squirt of her favourite perfume completed her weaponry. Now she felt as ready for battle as any of the Norman soldiers that may have stormed Framlingham Castle.

Confidently, she approached the shed, a brimming mug of coffee in each hand. Just as she got near the door and prepared to call to the boys to open it, it opened and a figure blundered out without looking and barged straight into her, jogging her arms and sending hot

36

coffee cascading down her clothes.

'Aaah!' Sophie screamed. 'You *idiot!*' Tears were in her eyes as she felt the hot liquid scalding through her leggings.

'Oh! Sorry. Well, how was *I* to know you were going to be outside the door?' said Ian, in aggrieved tones

'You should have looked. You weren't even *there* a minute ago.' She could cheerfully have strangled him. She really hated him. Apart from making her feel like a clumsy fool, he'd caused her to look like a drowned rat in front of Adrian. The smell of spilt coffee even cancelled out the perfume she'd put on specially. All her efforts wasted . . . it was an utter disaster!

Richard handed her an oily rag to wipe herself down with.

'*I'm* not a motorbike!' she said savagely, declining it. 'As for *you* — ' She turned on Ian and fixed him with a shrivelling look — 'you can come into the kitchen with me and make some more coffee, for your sins!'

She ignored Ian's forlorn attempts to apologize and stamped ahead of him into the kitchen looking back just once to make sure he was following her. Then she left him to it and went upstairs to change, furious tears blurring her eyes.

Tara was immersed in the game. She hardly looked up as Sophie came into the room, though after a moment she asked, 'Where's my coffee? You said you were making some.'

'Sorry. You can blame Ian,' Sophie said. 'I was just taking some into the shed for the boys when Ian came out and bashed into me. Completely drowned me in coffee. My leggings are ruined. I'll never get the stain out . . .'

Then she realized that Tara was laughing at her.

'I'm sorry about your leggings, I hope they'll wash OK. I do think it's funny, though. I wish I'd been there,' said Tara, giggling away.

If she knew the real circumstances, that all my efforts at impressing Adrian had been ruined, she wouldn't laugh, thought Sophie. I can't tell her, though . . . I can't.

She went back down to the kitchen, feeling in need of coffee herself, only to find Ian on the floor in a squatting position with a brush and dust-pan in his hand. He looked up guiltily as she came into the room.

'Dropped a mug. Sorry,' he said. 'It just slipped out of my hand.'

'Oh, no,' she groaned. 'Mum loved that mug. It's part of a set Richard and I gave her.'

She squatted down and tried to help him.

'Don't,' he said. 'You might cut yourself. The pieces are really sharp.'

She stood up and looked at him carefully sweeping up the pieces. She knew she had better say something. It wasn't like her to blow up the way she had. Richard especially must have thought her behaviour very odd.

'I'm sorry I was so nasty to you,' she said. 'It was just a bit of a shock, that's all. And I'd only just bought those leggings, so I was cross.'

'It's OK,' replied Ian. 'I seem to be in a clumsy phase today. Must be my bio-rhythms or something. I never thought anyone might be outside the door. It was just an accident.'

'Yes,' Sophie echoed. 'An accident. And I think I'm a bit stressed-out because of exams.'

'I know how you feel,' Ian said. 'I went through it all last year, don't forget. I was in a right old state until the results came through.'

He finished clearing up the debris, then poured boiling water into three new mugs. Sophie picked up two and carried them up to Richard's room. She handed one to Tara, who took a sip and screwed her face up in disgust.

'Ugh! Loads of sugar!' she reported.

Sophie realized she must have got the one destined for Adrian!

'I'll get you another,' she said.

She went back downstairs with the mug. When she went into the kitchen, she was thrilled to find Adrian standing there. It was a dream come true! Her heart beat faster and faster as the kitchen seemed to shrink to a tiny capsule containing just the two of them.

'This coffee was taking an awful long time to arrive so I came to see what had happened to it.' He gave Sophie a devastating smile.

She smiled back. In fact, her lips refused to obey any signals not to smile, they were jammed in an inane ear-to-ear grin. She knew she must look ridiculous. When she tried to force them into a speaking position, they went all wobbly.

'I . . . I think this is yours,' she said. 'I gave it to Tara by mistake.' Her voice didn't sound a bit like her own, it was all thin and ethereal, like Tinkerbell in a *Peter Pan* pantomime. Her whole face felt a mass of nervous twitches. He was so close to her! The surface of her skin itched, each tiny cell sensitized by his nearness. What if she were to reach out and touch him? Could her body stand the shock?

She didn't have to wait long to find out. She was still holding the mug. He took it from her and their hands touched slightly. Instantly, she felt a burning sensation where his skin had brushed hers. Oh, if this was love, it was an exquisite form of torture. She couldn't bear it, yet she wanted to prolong this moment for ever! But how?

Oh, stay here, Adrian, stay! Don't go back to the shed! she willed him.

'Ian broke a mug. Maybe he went to find Mum and apologize,' she said.

'He never used to be clumsy, but he is lately,' Adrian said. 'I don't know what's got into him. He's broken loads of things at home. Mum's wedding present vase . . . some glasses . . . He broke a mirror the other day. Seven years' bad luck! He

41

didn't like the idea of that much. I told him he'd better not start driving lessons yet, he'd wreck every car in the street!'

Cars . . . at last, a subject she could talk to him about. 'How's your new job going?' she enquired.

She wanted to know how many other people worked at the showroom — in particular, how many girls; but she knew she couldn't possibly ask that or he'd want to know why. Oh, he was looking so gorgeous! The top two buttons of his shirt were open, revealing a smooth, golden chest. She imagined planting a soft kiss in that hollow below his throat and felt herself blushing.

'The job's OK,' he said in reply to her question. 'I'm enjoying it. I think they like me. I might be able to get a really good car soon, too. They get trade-ins, people giving their car in part-exchange for a new one. I've got a few models in mind and I'm keeping a look-out. An old MGB or Midget would be nice, in racing green, or red. Ones in good nick are expensive, though. I want one that's falling apart, then I'll look out for the spares.'

There was a pause, during which Sophie prayed that Ian wouldn't come blundering back and ruin things. Adrian was gazing at her, looking her up and down. She felt quite embarrassed. When she'd peeled off her coffee-stained leggings, she'd changed into her jeans and now she wished she'd put on a skirt, or shorts. If he was going to examine her appearance quite so minutely, it was a shame she wasn't looking really good.

'I like your hair like that, it really suits you,' he said suddenly.

Sophie's mouth fell open and she knew she was blushing fierily now. 'Th-thank you,' she stammered. She looked away from him in confusion, but felt his eyes still on her as she opened a cupboard and looked for two more mugs. She took them out with unsteady hands and hoped she wouldn't be the cause of another breakage. She was racking her brains for something to say to him. Yet in a way she didn't want to say anything, in case there was another compliment coming her way — or, even better, an invitation to go out with him!

But suddenly, the interruption she had feared took place, though it was Tara in the doorway, not Ian.

'You've been gone for ages. I'm thirsty!' she said accusingly. 'I'm not interrupting anything, am I?' she asked, taking in the situation; a blushing Sophie, Ade standing close to her, and an atmosphere in the room that was charged and sizzling with hopes and unasked questions.

'No, of course not!' Sophie's tone was bright and false. *Please go away and leave us alone a bit longer*, were her true thoughts.

'Hi, Sis,' said Adrian. 'You look a sight this morning.'

'So do you. I hope you'll clean the shower after you've been in it,' Tara flung back.

Adrian in the shower . . . oh, what a wonderful, sinful thought! That tanned body under the running water . . . She mustn't think about such things.

'Sorry,' Sophie apologized to Tara. 'We just got talking.'

'I can see that. Now, where's that kettle?'

Tara took charge and in no time the two girls were back up in Richard's bedroom in front of the computer screen, with hot drinks and chocolate digestive biscuits.

'I think my big brother likes you,' Tara said.

Sophie felt as if a lightning bolt had

gone through her.

'Don't be daft!' she exclaimed. 'What on earth makes you think that?'

'Oh, just the way he looks at you. What do you think of him?'

'In what way?' asked Sophie, playing for time.

'As a potential boyfriend, I mean. Do you fancy him? Would you go out with him if he asked you?'

Sophie was suddenly finding it hard to breathe. 'It's awfully hot in here with the computer on,' she said, getting up to open the bedroom window.

'Stop avoiding the issue. Answer my question.' Tara's brown eyes were fixed on Sophie's face.

For a moment, Sophie wavered. Should she tell Tara? What would happen if she did? Would Tara help her get a date with Adrian? Or would it ruin their friendship? She thought of all the years the five of them had lived next door to one another; of the fun and friendship, the ups and downs, the worries and laughs they had all shared as neighbours. She didn't want to destroy that just because of some stupid fantasy of hers. The young prince on the castle wall, indeed! No. Far better to keep her feelings for Adrian a secret.

'I couldn't go out with Ade. I wouldn't dream of it. He's just your brother, and my next-door-neighbour, and that's all he'll ever be,' she lied.

How she managed to keep the blush inside, she'd never know. It was like a hot tide sweeping through her veins, a tide of guilt and longing.

'Oh,' Tara said. 'Never mind, then.'

'Never mind *what?*' Sophie cried.

Tara shrugged. 'Nothing,' she replied and insisted on changing the subject to boring old exams. Oh, if only they were over, thought Sophie desperately. If only she were free to spend hours alone with her thoughts. Free to go out. With Adrian . . . with anybody!

'I suppose we'd better get down to some work,' she said.

★ ★ ★

A few minutes later, as she waved Tara off through the gate in the fence, a thought kept nagging in her mind. What was Tara going to say that was so important? Had she been about to tell her that Adrian fancied her? How could she ever find out?

46

O! break my heart: poor bankrupt, break
at once!
To prison, eyes; ne'er look on liberty!

Shakespeare . . . now there was someone
who knew what an impossible love felt
like, Sophie mused. She wished she'd been
given *Macbeth* to study instead. Or
Physics and Chemistry. Oh, well. After
Monday, she'd never have to look at
Romeo and Juliet again!

5

Early that evening, after Sophie had got down to some hard revision and was feeling very pleased with herself, Tara came round again — dressed properly this time. In fact, thought Sophie, her neighbour was looking very pretty in pale blue shorts patterned with darker blue palm fronds and a short, clingy pale blue top. She wished with all her heart that she had been born with Tara's hair, a sheet of shimmering red-gold. Right now, it was held back from her face with two clips which emphasized the fact that she was wearing a touch of bronze eye-shadow.

It was a far cry from the slovenly-attired Tara of that morning, and Sophie wondered if she could possibly have a date which she had forgotten to mention — though that wouldn't be like gossipy Tara. Normally, she'd chatter about every little detail of her life. There hadn't been much action on the love-life front for some time, Sophie noted, putting it down to the strain of exams.

Many of her friends were breaking up with their boyfriends. Unable to see them because of the demands of revision, it led to tension and rows and many tearful phone calls. Sophie had had such a call that afternoon from Amy, a friend at school. She'd been going out with her boyfriend, Mark, for eight months and he had just chucked her, complaining that he hardly ever saw her any more.

Tara was looking glum. 'Guess what?' she said.

'What?' responded Sophie dutifully.

'Mum said it would be best to postpone my birthday party till after the exams.'

'Well, what's wrong with that? I think it's a much better idea. It only means waiting an extra week, and everyone will be much more in the mood for celebrating,' Sophie pointed out.

'Yes, I know, but it's not the same!' Tara pouted.

'Look,' said Sophie consolingly, 'we can still do something on your actual birthday.'

'Oh, yeah! That'll be a lot of fun — just you and me when we should be having a party!' Tara said scathingly.

'Well, if you don't want me to buy you a

drink . . . ' Sophie felt slightly wounded at Tara's immediate rejection of her suggestion.

'Sorry.' Tara reached out and squeezed her friend's shoulder. 'Don't take any notice of me. I've got exam-itis.'

'Me too. I never want to read another book as long as I live,' moaned Sophie.

'And I never want to have to think about another blasted science experiment. You're lucky. Poetry and plays are much easier to remember than Physics and Chemistry.'

'That's what *you* think!' Sophie retorted.

They continued comparing notes on exam subjects for some while, then the subject returned to that of Tara's birthday party. It was her sixteenth. A way to go before the big one, but nevertheless sixteen was well worth celebrating. It sounded — and felt — so very much older than fifteen.

'Who are you going to invite?' Sophie asked.

'Well, all the crowd from school, of course, and anyone you want to ask. And I hope Richard will come.' Although they lived next door to one another, they went to different schools. Tara was at a Catholic convent school and Sophie was at nearby Oakleigh High.

Richard? Sophie's sluggish, Adrian-obsessed ears pricked up at this. Why was Tara being so emphatic about Richard? Surely she didn't fancy him? She couldn't! It would be too terrible, having her fancy Tara's brother and Tara fancy hers!

But Tara continued, 'I want him to bring all his good-looking friends.' Sophie sagged with relief. That was all Richard was to Tara; a source of spare boys for the party. Thank goodness for that!

Then another, darker thought hit Sophie. What if Adrian brought a girl to the party? She couldn't stand that! How could she make sure it wouldn't happen? Then she had an idea.

'Talking of spare blokes,' Sophie said, 'don't you think we should ask our brothers not to bring any girlfriends to the party? Tell them we'll have lots of spare girls there needing partners for the evening.'

'It won't be a problem as far as Ian is concerned. I don't think he's *ever* had a girlfriend!' Tara said.

Sophie knew she shouldn't ask her next

question, but she simply had to. 'What about Ade?'

'Oh, *him*!' Tara snorted. 'You never know *who* he's going out with from one day to the next! I wish he'd settle down and just go out with one girl. I think it would do him good.'

'So do I,' said Sophie. Then, fearing she'd sounded too enthusiastic, she rapidly changed the subject to her own brother. 'Richard's as bad, but for different reasons. He's afraid to get involved in case he ends up at a university miles from home. He doesn't want to hurt anybody.'

'Aaah!' sighed Tara. 'I think that's really good of him. Ade's so different. He just revels in variety. Though it could be because he hasn't met one girl who's devastating enough to pin him down.'

Hmm, thought Sophie. *What about me? I'm sure I could be devastating enough for him, given half a chance.*

She saw her opportunity to pump Tara for information. 'Any idea what kind of girls Ade goes for?' she asked, trying to sound casual.

'He hasn't brought many home, but he seems to like blondes. And he says he likes lively girls with a cheeky sense of humour.

He can't stand dopey girls who have nothing to say.'

It's me, it's me! carolled Sophie's heart. *A blonde rinse and I'm everything he wants!* There and then, she determined to lighten her hair for the party.

Then Tara asked Sophie what kind of girls Richard liked, and she had to say, quite honestly, that she didn't know.

'Still, there'll be plenty for him to choose from at your party,' said Sophie, lightly.

'I suppose so,' said Tara. Rather abruptly, she tore a piece of paper out of a notebook and grabbed a pen. 'Right,' she said. 'Let's make a list. You, me, Richard and Ade. Who else?'

'And Ian,' Sophie added. 'We can't forget him.'

'No, I suppose we can't. But I'd like to sometimes,' said Tara.

'So would I!' agreed Sophie, and she wasn't thinking just about the spilled coffee. She was thinking about bicycles outside the library, Adrian and that blonde, and Ian's expression as he watched her face.

6

It was Friday afternoon and Sophie was at home trying to relax after sitting her History exam that morning. Feeling a need to do something physical for a change, she had washed a load of clothes in the washing machine and was now taking damp garments from the blue plastic laundry basket and pegging them out on the line. All at once, she sensed a prickling feeling up the back of her neck. Was someone watching her? A quick glance across the fence that divided the Thompson's garden from the Cassell's, revealed Ian, leaning against the wall by the back door.

'Hi,' she said.

'Hi,' he answered back. 'How are your exams going?'

'Deadly! I was OK on Ancient Rome this morning but I got the Crimean War mixed up and I'm sure I've failed Maths. I've always been hopeless at it, especially algebra. Dad said that in his day calculators hadn't been invented and they really *did* have to know how to work out fractions and things. But I really don't see why *we* have to know.'

'In case your batteries fail, I suppose,' Ian said.

'I feel as though mine have failed at the moment. Utterly drained. Not an ounce of life left in them,' declaimed Sophie dramatically.

'I'm glad I'm only doing mocks this year. You'll feel better once it's all over. It'll be like a ton weight lifted off your shoulders,' Ian said.

'A ton weight lifted off my stomach is what I need. I must have put on stones since I've been swotting. I can't stop eating biscuits,' Sophie confided.

Ian looked her up and down, a serious expression on his face. 'You look fine to me,' he said.

'Thanks,' Sophie replied. Why couldn't it have been Adrian who'd said that? She would have taken it as a bigger compliment then. If only she and Adrian could chat as easily as she and Ian did. If only she didn't feel completely tongue-tied the moment Adrian appeared!

'I'm looking forward to the party,' Ian said.

'So am I,' another voice chimed in. Adrian's!

It was almost a week since that encounter in the kitchen — a week in which she had been too caught up in exam-fever to spare much thought for anyone, even Adrian. She hadn't glimpsed him once during the week. But now he was there, she felt the roller-coaster feelings come bumping back to the pounding of her heartbeat.

'Are you planning to drag Richard away from his studies again tonight?' she asked boldly. 'You shouldn't, you know. He was so wrecked after last Friday night that he could hardly do any work all day Saturday. What *did* the two of you get up to?' She tried to make her voice sound jokey and teasing, to mask her serious intent.

Ian interrupted at that moment by saying, 'See you,' and disappearing indoors. Sophie hoped it wouldn't distract Adrian from answering her question.

It didn't. 'Dunno. Can't remember,' he said cheerfully. How infuriating! She hadn't found out a thing.

Adrian shrugged and changed the subject. 'Are you doing anything tonight?'

56

he asked casually.

Here it comes, Sophie thought. *The big date at last!* Her heart was thumping so hard that it was vibrating her whole body and she felt faint. Somehow, she managed to keep her cool and echoed his shrug with one of her own. 'Don't think so,' she said.

'I've got two free tickets for a comedy night at 'Jesters'.' 'Jesters' was a venue in town which had bands some nights and comedy on others. Stand-up comedians weren't really her thing, but she was prepared to try anything if it was with Adrian. She was even starting to look forward to it when he continued, 'I thought you and Tara might like to use them.'

'Oh!' Her shock must have shown on her face.

He laughed. 'What's up, Sophe? Not in a laughing mood?'

She recovered herself quickly. 'No. Not really. Not after this morning's exam. And I don't think Tara . . . '

She let her voice tail off. Talk about her batteries running down! She felt absolutely exhausted with disappointment. It was like a huge mountain crushing down on her. What a fool she had been, to think that Adrian might want to go out with her. When he'd told her how nice she looked last Saturday, it must have meant nothing. It was just something to say. Politeness. Chitchat. What a fool she had been to read so much into it.

'Well, better go in, I suppose. I've got lots to do,' she said.

'I don't often see you alone to talk to you,' he said and *whammo!* — all those excited feelings came thumping back. She stood still, electrified.

'I've been noticing you a lot recently,' he continued. 'How you've grown up. How you've changed.'

'How do you mean?' she asked, trying to sound calm and only vaguely interested when she was quivering with curiosity and excitement. Trust Adrian to go and surprise her again! Every time she started to give up on him and think her longing for him was impossible, he would say something to fan the flames of hope and get her dreaming those dreams again.

'You used to be a tiny little thing with hair like a dandelion clock,' he said.

'What am I now, then?' she asked with bated breath.

He grinned teasingly. 'Well . . . a *bigger*

thing with hair like a double dandelion clock!'

'Oh!' she exclaimed exasperatedly.

His grin moved up a notch into a full-throated laugh. 'No, seriously,' he said, 'you've got really pretty. And I'm not the only one who's noticed.'

'Oh? Who are all the others, then?' she asked, knowing she was flirting with him. Oh, wow! This was bliss! She'd never felt so happy. Adrian fancied her! Not only that, so did some of his friends, and maybe that had made Adrian feel a tiny bit jealous. Maybe it was one of his friends saying, 'Your next-door neighbour's a bit of all right,' or something like that, that had prodded him into action. She knew only too well how boys talked about girls, from listening to Richard's friends.

Adrian just grinned and refused to elaborate. Sophie didn't care. She was floating somewhere on a cloud way above the garden. He was working up to asking her out. Any second now . . .

There was the sound of a window opening above her head. 'Ade? Ade!'

Then Richard leaned out of his bedroom window and called, 'Hey, Ade! Stop chatting up my sister and come and cheer me up. All this revising's driving me barmy!'

Oh, no! Sophie could have killed him. How could he interrupt right now, at the most important moment in her life?

Adrian glanced at his watch, a big, complicated contraption with all kinds of dials and knobs on it, set on a wide, black, perforated rubber strap. 'Just for ten minutes. Then I've got to be somewhere,' he said.

He let himself in through the gate in the fence, which had been put in when the families first became friends, then strode past Sophie, through the kitchen door and into the Thompson's house as if he owned it, leaving her standing dejectedly amongst the washing hanging damply from the line.

Boys! she exploded to herself. You just never knew where you stood with them. But she felt she was getting somewhere, albeit very slowly. And she had a sneaky hunch that something just might happen at Tara's party.

★ ★ ★

Four days went by; four days of hard work, sitting exams and not seeing even a glimpse of Adrian. Richard's exams were over before Sophie's. She glowered at him as he came slamming into the house on Friday afternoon, yelling, 'Hooray! Freedom!' and hurling an armful of books across the living-room.

'It's all right for some,' she grunted, biting savagely into a peanut-butter sandwich.

As soon as she'd done so, she wished she hadn't. How on earth would she squeeze herself into the cream-coloured dress she'd bought for Tara's party if she was all fat and bulgy? She had chosen it from her mother's catalogue and she wished she hadn't chosen cream now, because dark colours made you look slimmer. She'd seen Tara's outfit, a black velvet shorts suit which made her stunning hair look even redder and her legs look long and slender. Why had she gone and bought that dress? Why hadn't she chosen something sexy like Tara? She was going to look a real frump by comparison.

'I suppose you're going to go out and get wrecked tonight,' she grumbled.

'You bet!' Richard answered cheerfully.

'With Ade?' Sophie ventured.

'If he's around. You know Ade!'

61

Wish I knew him a bit better, thought Sophie wistfully.

Richard got on the phone and rounded up some of his mates. When one of them, Darrell, came round, Richard took him next door to collect Ade. Why couldn't he have arranged for Adrian to call round at their house? Instead, he had deprived Sophie of a chance to see him.

★ ★ ★

She spent the whole weekend swotting up on Geography and French, but she didn't mind because it was her last weekend of hard work. Next weekend — Tara's birthday party!

7

Tara's party was due to start at eight. Sophie hadn't been able to eat a thing all day. Was this destined to be the night Adrian took her in his arms and kissed her, out in the garden under the stars? She prayed to any guardian angel or fairy-godmother who might be listening, to please make it so.

Food was set out on the dining-table, drinks on the table in the kitchen. There were French loaves, pâté and cheese, sausage rolls, lots of things on sticks, plates of sandwiches kept fresh beneath cling-film, plus beer, wine, cider and lots of mineral water and soft drinks. Anything stronger had been banned.

Their parents had promised to stay next door, trusting Ade, as the eldest, to keep his eye on proceedings.

'I think Dad wants to make sure no one nicks his darts trophy. I *mean*! Who'd want that old thing?' scoffed Tara.

The fake tan she had rubbed on to her pale limbs the day before had worked slightly, and Sophie felt a little less pallid in her cream dress. Tara had gone one better and treated her long legs to three coats so they were now a glorious, eye-catching tan. Whoever she might have her eye on, she couldn't fail to pull them in that outfit, with those legs, Sophie thought enviously.

She had gone next door to help Tara set things up. Adrian was out, unfortunately, having gone somewhere with his dad. Now it was ten-past-seven and she was back home getting changed and was sure she'd never get her hair and make-up right. The hand that held the mascara brush was trembling so that she kept putting splodges on her face, having to wipe it off and start again. But at last she felt she was as ready as she would ever be. She had butterflies in her tummy. It was almost eight o'clock!

Tara and Sophie couldn't have made a greater contrast as they stood greeting guests, one in a tiny, clingy black outfit that showed all her legs, Sophie in a long cream outfit that swept down to ankle level, though it did have buttons up the front, undone to just above knee level. Ian was being very useful, pouring drinks and showing people where to put their coats. He's looking good tonight, Sophie thought with a slight shock. In a dazzling white shirt and black jeans, with his hair brushed and gelled till it gleamed like the coat of a well-groomed chestnut pony, he looked . . . well, almost handsome. She had to blink to remind herself that it was, after all, only Ian.

By nine, two males were conspicuous by their absence; Richard and Adrian. Sophie was really agitated. An hour later they still hadn't shown up. At ten-thirty, Tara turned the music up loud and Ian agreed to act as DJ. Still no Adrian or Richard.

It was nearly eleven before they rolled in. They brought some of their friends with them, all slightly the worse for wear, but all in the party spirit. Those girls who hadn't yet paired off with anybody perked up and rushed excitedly upstairs to comb their hair and apply fresh make-up at the thought of a new selection of boys to choose from.

Sophie felt slightly detached from it all. She was leaning against the wall sipping fruit punch, which one of the boys had laced with vodka, when she felt the warmth of another body standing close to hers. She turned round and nearly dropped her cup on the carpet. It was Adrian and, what was more, he was sliding his arm around her shoulders.

'Help me stand up!' he said.

'You're not that drunk, surely?' Sophie replied scoldingly, but there was humour in her tone.

'Even if I was stone-cold sober, I'd still like to put my arm round you,' he said.

Sophie felt her face melt and her entire body followed suit. She felt as if she were one big happy smile.

'Let's dance,' Adrian murmured, taking her cup off her and placing it on the bookshelf, then leading her to a space near the mantelpiece.

At first they danced without touching. Sophie's long dress forced her to move differently from usual. Instead of her normal energetic way of dancing, she had to swivel and glide, one bare, golden-brown knee poking suggestively out of the unbuttoned skirt of her dress. Pretending to glance down at the rug she was standing on, she surreptitiously undid another couple of buttons.

'I've never seen you looking as good as you do tonight,' Adrian said.

Sophie shot him a wide-eyed glance, wondering if he was just being polite or — even worse — joking. But his face was completely serious and as his eyes met Sophie's, he gave her a grin which suddenly turned up the heat in the stuffy room by at least ten degrees. He reached out and she felt him take hold of her hands. Then she was pulled towards him . . . and against him. Before she had time to draw breath, his lips were nearing hers.

There was a brief moment which seemed to last for eternity when his lips were so close to hers that she could feel the warmth of them, but their mouths hadn't yet touched. She held her breath, feeling as if she were suspended in space. Her eyes closed and she instinctively tilted her face up to his. His hands slid either side of her face, burying themselves in her hair. His hard thighs were pressing against hers. She was going to fall over! But he moved one hand and encircled the small of her back with his arm, pulling her even closer to him.

And then their lips met and a million zingy tingles shot through Sophie, like sherbert fizzing in her veins. That first kiss was a warm, still pressure of mouth on mouth. Then he moved back from her and smiled.

'That was nice!' he said. 'I've been wanting to do that for ages!'

'Same here,' Sophie answered, her voice breathy with nerves. She cast a wild glance round the room to see if Tara had noticed. She couldn't see her anywhere.

Then she was kissed for a second time — a kiss that was wildly, expertly different. It started with Adrian gently sucking her lower lip between his. He let it go, then ran his tongue inside her upper lip, making her feel all tickly and shivery. Then came the kiss to end all kisses, a full-blown explosion of passion, pressing together, room and people forgotten, time standing still.

They broke from it, trembling. They gazed at each other. A smear of Sophie's lipstick was on Adrian's chin. She put up a shaky finger and wiped it off, joking about the shade not suiting him. They carried on dancing but everything had changed. Sophie's life had changed. She knew she was moving differently. Her stiff, awkward dancing had become fluid and graceful. She felt at one with the music . . . at one with everything from the chair in the corner, to the carpet beneath her feet, to the trees out in the garden. A life-force was flowing through her, connecting her to something out there beyond everything. If this was love . . . well, if it was, it was pure, utter, transforming magic.

She wondered if anyone else had noticed the change in her. She felt as radiant as the sun. But around her people were dancing and chatting as normal. Nobody was looking at her in any unusual way. She noticed that Richard was dancing with Carol-Ann Davidson. Not just dancing, either; their bodies and lips were pressed together and their feet performing the merest rhythmic shuffle.

Is that how we looked when we were kissing? Sophie wondered. Wrapped up in a world of our own, oblivious to anything? Where was Tara? Feeling a sudden urge to re-familiarize herself with normality, she said, 'Excuse me a mo,' and went into the kitchen, expecting to find Tara in there chatting to friends. But she wasn't.

Maybe she's gone up to the bathroom, Sophie thought. She went upstairs and joined the queue for the loo. Tara wasn't in it and the person who came out of the bathroom wasn't her, either.

She tapped on Tara's bedroom door. There was no sound from inside so she went in. Tara was sitting at her dressing-table. She had a tissue in her hand and was blotting her left eye. She turned as she heard Sophie. There was a flash of something hostile on her face — anger, defiance . . . something. Sophie was puzzled. But Tara's face cleared on seeing who it was, and she grinned.

'I got something in my eye,' she explained. 'I was trying to get it out.'

Tara's eyes looked pink-rimmed and devoid of make-up. 'It could have been the smoke,' she said. Some of the guests were smoking even though she had asked them to go outside and do it.

Sophie sat on the edge of the bed and watched Tara re-apply her eye make-up.

'How do you think the party's going? Do you think everyone's enjoying them-selves?' Tara asked her.

'It's great!' Sophie said brightly. Should she tell Tara about Adrian? The news was bubbling away inside her. She wanted to tell the whole world! 'Richard looks as though he's having a good time. That Carol-Ann girl's all over him like a rash.'

'Oh,' said Tara, sounding completely

uninterested. 'How about Ian? Has he got off with anybody yet?'

'No. He's still playing DJ,' said Sophie. 'It's a shame he won't drag himself away from the stereo. He's looking quite tasty tonight, for him.'

'Guess who had to iron his shirt?' said Tara.

'Isn't he capable of doing it himself?' snorted Sophie.

'Of course he is, but you know boys . . . Talking of which, how's Adrian getting on?'

A tidal wave of crimson spread over Sophie's cheeks. 'Er . . . um . . . ' she muttered, her lips twisting into a guilty grin.

'You don't mean . . . No, I don't believe it! You and Ade?' Tara looked quite shocked.

'Um, yes. He asked me to dance and then . . . he kissed me.'

'Oh. Did he, indeed!'

Tara didn't sound entirely pleased and Sophie was puzzled. There was a strange undercurrent in the room; had been ever since she came in. She caught an odd expression on Tara's face. What was going on?

'Oh, it's nothing,' Sophie said dismissively. 'I'm sure he doesn't mean anything

71

by it. It's just a bit of party fun.' As she spoke the words, she sincerely hoped they weren't true.

'Well, you know Ade. I wouldn't like to think of you getting hurt, Sophie,' Tara said. 'As long as you can accept that that's probably all it is . . . party fun. Never say I didn't warn you.' She gave Sophie a candid look.

Sophie bit her lip and looked away. 'I . . . I'd better get back down,' she said. 'Are you coming?'

'I'll follow you in a minute,' Tara said.

As Sophie closed the bedroom door, she realized she couldn't get downstairs fast enough. She had an awful fear that she would find Adrian dancing with — or, even worse, kissing — another girl. *Party fun*, indeed! She, Sophie Thompson, was not going to be looked upon as mere party fun — not in a million years!

As she descended the stairs, threading her way with difficulty between the couples who were lounging all over them, she saw Adrian standing in the hall. His face lit up when he saw her.

'I was beginning to think you'd gone home!' he said.

He took her hand and led her into the

kitchen where he poured them each a white wine spritzer.

'Cheers!' he said, raising his cup.

She wanted to say, 'To us,' but it seemed presumptuous so she just smiled.

'Isn't it strange?' he said.

'What is?' she responded.

'That we've lived next door to each other all this time and only just kissed.'

'Mmm,' she replied, thinking, *what's going to happen now?*

'I've fancied you for ages,' he said.

And me you, she thought, but didn't want to inflate his ego by telling him. Her mind suddenly flashed back to that vision on the castle wall and her heart gave a little jump. That wonderful fantasy was now within her grasp!

'Shall we go out together one night?' he asked her.

'Yes, that would be nice.' What tame words to express the rich depths of emotion she was feeling. But instinct told her to be cautious and not reveal everything right at the start. She didn't want to frighten him off by making him think she was too keen.

'A film? Yes?' he said.

'Yes.' She hadn't been to the cinema for

ages, she'd been working too hard. Suddenly, it dawned on her that those days were in the past, temporarily at least. No more exams. A whole summer of freedom — and Adrian!

8

The morning after the party, Sophie slept in. She woke at twenty-to-eleven to find sunlight streaming through a chink at the top of the curtain. Then, with a shock, the events of the previous night leaped back into her brain. Adrian! She'd kissed Adrian! She'd got a date with him! She sat up, crossed her arms and hugged herself. Oh, it was so fantastic . . . so absolutely, unbelievably thrilling!

Their cinema trip had been arranged for Monday evening and Adrian was going to call for her at seven-thirty. Sophie did a quick calculation; thirty-three-and-a-half hours to wait. It seemed like a lifetime.

When she got up and went downstairs, Richard was sitting at the table in the dining end of their big through-lounge, reading a Sunday paper. He had his feet propped on the polished surface of the dining-table and swung them off guiltily as Sophie approached.

'So how's Carol-Ann? Got a date?' Sophie asked him.

'I might ask you the same thing,' Richard replied, giving her an exaggerated wink.

'About Carol-Ann? I don't fancy dating her, she's not my type,' said Sophie, sarcastically.

'Have you or haven't you got a date with Adrian?' Richard asked, ignoring his sister's attempt at a joke.

'Maybe I have . . . ' she said.

'And maybe I have a date, too. When's yours?' asked Richard.

'Tomorrow,' Sophie said.

'That's good. I'm glad it's not tonight. I want Ade to come over to Simon's house with me. Simon's cousin's taken his old motorbike apart and he might sell me a few parts for mine, but I want a second opinion. Ade's a bit more mechanical than me.' Richard paused, then added, 'He should be getting his new car this week. Did he tell you about it?'

'No, he didn't. But it was a bit too noisy at the party to do much talking,' said Sophie.

'So I noticed!' said Richard, teasingly.

'I don't know how. You looked much too busy to be taking any notice of anything,' Sophie teased back, good-humouredly.

She and her brother were used to this kind of banter. It had been going on all their lives. They were always pulling each other's legs about things but Sophie would never have dreamt of saying or doing anything really nasty to him, or he to her. Richard may have found Sophie an annoying little sister at times, but he was too easy-going and good-humoured to stay upset or annoyed for long.

Which was why, when he *did* say something serious, Sophie was inclined to take notice.

'You know, Sophe, I wouldn't automatically believe everything Ade says,' Richard announced. Sophie froze, suddenly hearing him very clearly indeed. 'Take it all with a pinch of salt.'

'What do you mean? Take *what* with a pinch of salt?' She could feel her happiness draining away and she grabbed on to it desperately, trying to hold it in her heart.

'Whatever,' Richard said enigmatically, going back to his paper. And no matter how much she tried to get him to say more, he refused to open up on the subject, merely remarking that he knew Ade better than she did.

Oh, damn, thought Sophie as she went into the kitchen in search of breakfast. Why did he have to go and spoil things? She knew what he was hinting at. Adrian went out with a lot of girls and Richard, concerned for her, didn't want to see her make a fool of herself, or end up with a broken heart.

But she wouldn't. Her heart was quite safe. She was sensible. She wouldn't hand Adrian her innermost feelings on a plate. Not until he'd offered his. If he were to say, 'I love you,' she knew what her response would be. But she wouldn't say a word until he had spoken first.

With that decision firmly made, Sophie was able to chomp into her bowl of cereal with gusto — and polish off three pieces of toast and honey.

★   ★   ★

Tara came round in the early evening. She had her friend Janey with her. 'Where's Richard?' Tara enquired.

'He and Adrian have gone to look at motorbike parts,' Sophie informed her.

Tara grimaced. 'Typical,' she grunted. She didn't seem in the best of moods.

'What's this about Ade getting a new car?' asked Janey, settling her long limbs into an arm-chair in the lounge and teasing out her black curls with her fingers.

'Yes, I was going to ask you about that,' Sophie added. 'Do you know what he's getting?'

'A BMW,' declared Tara.

'No!' said Sophie.

'Wow!' said Janey. 'But they cost a fortune! My dad's got one.'

'Oh, it's not a new one, it's a second-hand one that's been done up by the firm he works for,' Tara explained.

'Even so . . . ' Janey breathed. Her eyes were shining. Sophie realized that she was part of the legion of women who fancied Adrian and a little thrill rippled through her. Janey might fancy him but she, Sophie, was going out with him!

'When's he getting it?' Sophie asked.

'Tomorrow, I think.'

Tomorrow . . . that was when they were having their first date. So she would be picked up and chauffeured to the cinema in a brand spanking new — well, spanking second-hand — BMW! That really was style, Sophie thought. She imagined Adrian at the wheel, looking ultra-cool in a white shirt and shades, with herself at his side, in that cream dress she wore for the party. Oh, yes, this was the life she wanted!

Tara and Janey were talking about something, but Sophie wasn't listening. She was off in a world of her own, a world in which she and Adrian were driving along the French Riviera like film stars, their progress charted by movie and television cameras. They would be such a glamorous couple that they would be offered their own television series to star in. Their marriage . . . their *marriage!* . . . would take up several pages in *Hello!*

Sophie's ears suddenly tuned in to a name she recognized: Richard. Janey was talking about Carol-Ann.

'She rang me this morning. She's dead keen, you know. Apparently she's been after him for ages,' Janey said.

'Well, good luck to her,' said Tara brusquely. Turning to Sophie, she enquired, 'What do you think her chances are, Sophie?'

'Dunno.' Sophie gave a shrug. 'Richard's worried about committing himself to anyone because of going off to university. I suppose you can see his point.'

'Yes,' said Tara. 'That makes sense.' She appeared to have brightened up all of a sudden. 'Well . . . ' She got to her feet. 'Let's not waste the evening sitting around. Let's go out. Shall we see who's down at 'Joe's'?'

'Joe's Caff', spelt just like that, was the local hang-out for a lot of their friends. At least, thought Sophie, it will help to pass the awful waiting time between now and tomorrow night.

★ ★ ★

At seven-twenty on Monday evening, Sophie decided to change her entire outfit. The cream dress just didn't seem right for a trip to the cinema. Instead, she put on her beige linen trousers, a brown sleeveless T-shirt and a long, floaty linen waistcoat with white embroidery. She fastened her hair back in a band. Then, breathlessly, she consulted her watch. One minute to go! Her heart was pounding excitedly and her hands felt clammy. She wiped them on her trousers. Have I got enough perfume on?

81

she wondered. She reached agitatedly for the spray, thinking, *He'll be here any moment!*

But he wasn't. Seven-thirty-five came and went. A quarter-to-eight . . . ten-to . . . they were going to miss the start of the film!

Sophie's bedroom was at the back of the house. Her parents had the large room at the front. She went in and peered out of the window. The rays of the setting sun streaked the sky and a blackbird was singing deafeningly on a tree branch near the window. There was no BMW parked in the street.

Maybe she should call next door . . . But that would make her seem too eager. Perhaps he'd got back from work late and was even now showering and changing and planning his apology.

When a quarter-past-eight came and went, Sophie went up to her room and slumped down on her bed. There was a lump of grief and defeat in her throat that was too big to swallow. It was choking her. The only way of dissolving it was by crying, but she didn't want to. She didn't want him to come round and catch her red-eyed and tearful. She still held on to a last ray of hope. He would still come. No matter how late it was, he would come round, even if it was only to apologize. He wouldn't stand her up on their very first date. He *couldn't*!

9

But he did. By eleven, Sophie finally admitted defeat. She didn't have to take her make-up off — she cried it off. Then she angrily tugged off her clothes, threw them into a crumpled heap on the carpet and crawled into bed, where she wept until she had a headache and was so exhausted that she finally slept.

★   ★   ★

She awoke next day, determined never, ever to speak to Adrian Cassell again. She would ignore him completely. When she went next door to see Tara, she would pretend Adrian didn't exist. Scum like him didn't *deserve* to exist!

She washed, bathed her sore, dry eyes, dressed and went out of the house, preparing to stride smartly in an 'I don't care' way down the street in the direction of the newsagent's, to buy a Diet Coke and a magazine. All the houses in Pevensey Crescent had front gardens.

Parked right outside the Thompson's front gate was a car Sophie had never seen before. It was a shiny black BMW. Her heart missed a beat. The creep! So he'd got his car last night and hadn't taken her out in it!

She set her chin high and strode down the road. It was just gone eight o'clock. Any time now Adrian would be setting off for work. If she lingered on the way back, she could bump into him 'accidentally on purpose' and see what his reaction was . . . whether he gave a convincing enough explanation for last night. She wasn't sure if she would forgive him, even if his explanation *was* convincing. Standing a girl up on a first date was pretty unforgivable. She would have to wait and see.

She made her purchases quickly, then walked very slowly back along the road, staring at every car that went past. But she didn't see Adrian. She couldn't stand by her front gate all morning so, reluctantly, she went in.

When she went out later, the car was still there and she realized Adrian must have gone to work without it.

Suddenly, instead of a glorious summer

of love and happiness stretching ahead of her, her horizon clouded over and a black mood descended. Weeks and empty weeks loomed ahead. How was she going to fill them? There was talk of her parents taking a week off work so that they could rent a cottage in Wales, which is what they had always done when Richard and Sophie were younger. Richard was quite adamant that he was now too old for that kind of holiday and he wanted to go abroad, to Ibiza or a Greek island. Sophie had no plans. Yesterday, holidays hadn't mattered. In fact, they would have been an intrusion into the glorious love-affair she had planned. Now, any distraction would be welcome, even a wet week in Wales!

When she got in, Richard was sitting at the kitchen table, eating a hearty fry-up.

'Oh, hi, you're up,' he said. 'I've got a message from Ade for you. Says he's very sorry about the movies. It's my fault, really. I went to meet him after work, to have a look at the car. Then I talked him into going for a drive. And then we found ourselves in Kelverton, and you know that little pub by the river, 'The Roebuck'? Well, we ended up in there. Low-alcohol lager, naturally. Sitting by the river, watching the sun go down. And then this really good folksy band started playing. Then suddenly it was closing time. I assured Ade that you wouldn't mind too much. It's not like he's a stranger, after all. We *have* all known each other for ever — I mean, it's not like he's a proper boyfriend. I said you'd forgive him and it would be OK to make it another night. Did I do the right thing?'

Looking at Sophie's miserable face, Richard's expression changed as he suddenly cottoned on to the gravity of the situation.

'Oh, dear,' he said worriedly. 'I didn't do the right thing, did I? Look, I'm terribly sorry, Sophe. It *was* all my fault. I thought a movie could wait — that there were plenty more nights. I didn't realize you'd set your heart on it being last night.'

'It's . . . it's OK.' Sophie shrugged and forced herself to smile, though she was seething inwardly. Not a proper boyfriend, indeed! 'I know how these things can happen,' she went on. 'But you *knew* we had a date, Richard. How *could* you?'

Richard's open, honest face adopted a hopeless, hang-dog expression. 'I really am sorry, Sophie. What can I do to make it up to you?' he said.

'Nothing. I shouldn't have looked forward to it so much. I might have known something would go wrong,' she said. 'Now, I really must have a coffee.'

'He says he'll ring you from work today,' Richard added.

Suddenly, the world was a brighter place. Though she couldn't quite forgive Richard for distracting Adrian, or Adrian for not ringing her from the pub to explain. Surely he realized that a phone call was just plain courtesy?

Feeling more cheerful now that she understood what had happened, she hummed to herself as she waited for the kettle to boil. Everything was OK, after all. In an odd sort of way the postponement of their date suited her in as much as it wasn't over and she still had it to look forward to.

* * *

It took place that very evening. At five, the phone went and it was Adrian, ringing her from work.

'Sorry about last night,' he said. 'It was very bad of me. I hope you can forgive me.

88

Do you still want to come out with me after this?'

'I think I might just manage it,' Sophie said, aware of a chuckle in her voice.

'Right,' said Adrian. 'How about tonight, then, if you've got nothing planned?'

Sophie hadn't. Of course she hadn't!

He said he'd come round for her at seven and they could go for a bite to eat before the film, which started at eight-thirty. To her disappointment, he said he didn't want to take the car as there was nowhere to park near the cinema, and he fancied having a drink afterwards. Sophie thought it was a bit of a come-down, having to take a bus when there was a wonderful car sitting there unused, but being with Adrian was the most important thing. It wouldn't really have mattered if he'd taken her there in an ice-cream van as long as he was next to her, exuding that fresh, tangy cologne and all those sexy vibes.

There had been a quick, sharp shower and now every garden thrust its mingled scents into the breezy air. Sophie sniffed appreciatively. She was wearing the same outfit she had been going to wear last night and, oddly enough, she and Adrian almost looked like twins, as he was wearing loose beige trousers and a linen waist-coat, too. When she'd opened the door to him, he'd said, 'Snap!'

As she walked along next to him, she felt confident, on top of the world, glad to be alive. It felt like the summit of everything she had ever tried to achieve. This must be what it felt like to land a top job, or win the lottery.

'You look happy,' he commented. 'Penny for them.'

She couldn't tell him the truth, that he was the reason for her smile, so she just said, 'Well, it's the end of exams, the beginning of the holidays . . . of *course* I'm feeling happy!'

There was a small café next to the cinema. They ordered coffee and toasted sandwiches but Sophie just nibbled at hers, unable to taste it. She was too excited to eat, though she drank her *cappuccino*, then surreptitiously wiped her mouth in case she had a moustache of froth.

The cinema was half empty. She hoped for one mad instant that Adrian would lead her into the back row, but he didn't.

Instead, he went half-way down and led her into the centre of a row, where there was no one sitting in front. They settled into their seats and the film began, but Sophie's attention wasn't on the screen, it was all on Adrian. She was so aware of him next to her that the whole side of her body beside him was tingling, as if she had pins and needles. He shifted his leg, and his knee briefly touched hers.

Oh, why won't you leave it there? she thought, feeling her skin buzz where the brief contact had been.

'Good, isn't it?' he murmured during a pause in the action.

'Yes,' she answered breathily, hoping he wouldn't want to start a detailed discussion about the plot when she hadn't been concentrating on the film in the slightest. It was a shame; she had been looking forward to seeing this particular film. But how on earth could she lose herself in it when the boy who had caused her three whole months of yearning and hoping was at last here by her side? No wonder she couldn't stop her legs trembling slightly. No wonder she was breathing so quickly and shallowly, and felt dizzy, as if she were a bit drunk.

Oh, Adrian, I love you so much, she thought, feeling the emotion rising up to her throat. If only he would just reach for her hand!

As if he had picked up her wish telepathically, he suddenly went one better than hand-holding and slid his arm along the back of her seat so that it draped itself round her shoulders.

Something snapped inside her, a great release of tension. She let out a sigh and sagged against him, snuggling as close as she could get, fitting her left shoulder into his armpit and resting her head on his shoulder. She felt his lips nuzzle her forehead. Then they softly kissed the bridge of her nose and she turned her face so that her lips were offered to his.

He took them. She felt the faintest warm, moist whisper of a kiss brushing against her lips. Her eyes were tightly closed and she was aware of strong-coloured lights playing on her eyelids, reflected from the cinema screen.

'Little Sophie,' he murmured against her mouth, his lips tickling hers. She smiled and his lips came down again, this time more forcefully. A sudden loud burst of gunfire from the movie sound-track made her jump. He laughed and squeezed his arm tightly round her, holding her safe, refusing to let her go as his kiss became more demanding.

Now they were kissing for real. It was sheer heaven, even better than at the party because it was more private, sitting here in the darkness, and she didn't feel at all self-conscious. His exploring tongue . . . his sweet, slightly pepperminty breath . . . the way their mouths and faces moved together, in perfect timing, like dancers . . . it was bliss.

Neither of them saw any more of the film. They remained locked together, mouths joined, and only broke apart when the lights went up. Sophie was so dazed, she couldn't stand. She just sat there grinning weakly, knowing her hair was all messed up. Adrian's was too, sticking up in spiky bits where her fingers had raked through it.

'Phew!' he exclaimed, trying to flatten it down. He gave Sophie a grin that tugged at her heart, a perplexed 'what have you done to me?' type of grin.

'Enjoy it?' he asked.

Sophie didn't know whether he meant the film, or their kiss, so she just went,

'Mmm,' and nodded and let him take her hand and tug her to her feet.

There was a pub across the street to the cinema. Sophie couldn't feel the pavement beneath her feet. It felt as if she were floating above the ground like a hovercraft. The interior of the pub was a dizzying babble of lights and noise. Sophie clutched the edge of the bar for support and leaned against Adrian, hoping every girl in the pub was envying her. *We look as if we belong together*, she thought. *We look a co-ordinated couple. We look as if we've been together for ages.*

She ordered a fizzy orange and he had a pint of lager. They found a table next to the doors which led out to the pub garden. Coloured lights draped the trees, giving a fairy-tale effect and a bright half moon sailed in a cloudless night sky.

'Pretty, isn't it?' said Adrian. He reached out and placed his hand over hers on the table-top. She wanted this moment to last for ever. He stroked her hand gently, then picked it up, carried it to his lips and planted a soft kiss on each finger-tip in turn.

Sophie had never had her fingers kissed before. She felt as if she had been transported back through the centuries. She was Lady Sophie and he was Sir Adrian, a knight of the Round Table who was going off to fight dragons for her.

'You're very quiet tonight. Not at all like your normal chatty self,' Adrian observed.

What could she say? She really was lost for words, adrift on a tide of pure sensation. She smiled. 'What shall we talk about?' she said. 'Please don't say motorbikes!'

'How about my new car, then?'

'It looks wonderful,' Sophie said. 'I was rather hoping I'd get a chance to ride in it.'

'Next time,' Adrian promised.

Sophie's heart leaped. So there *was* going to be a next time!

* * *

And there was, just two days later. He said he'd ring her and he was true to his word. Now it was Thursday and at last her wish to ride in the BMW was to be fulfilled!

'Your chauffeur, Madam!' joked Adrian, settling himself at the steering-wheel. 'And where would Madam like to be taken?'

'Madam would like . . . Oh, I know! How about taking me to that pub you went to with Richard? 'The Roebuck'? I liked the sound of that.'

Adrian agreed and soon they were swishing through the countryside. *This is the life!* thought Sophie, relaxing in the leather seat. *This year a BMW . . . next year a Mercedes. And then — a Rolls Royce!*

They spent a magical evening in the pub. Sophie soon forgot her nerves and chatted away to Adrian just like she had always done. Except that there was a difference, a kind of zing in the air, a memory of their kisses, a longing for more.

On the way back, Adrian took a left turn, slowed down and stopped. 'It's a beautiful night,' he said. 'Shall we go for a walk?'

There was a sign indicating a footpath. They walked single-file down an over-grown lane and reached a stile. Adrian went over first and held out his hand to help Sophie. She was wearing a long skirt and in her efforts to look elegant and climb over the top bar, she caught her foot and went tumbling on top of Adrian. He landed on his back on the grass with a thump and, for a moment, was silent.

'Are you all right?' Sophie asked anxiously, feeling for his face in the darkness. Now that they were at ground level beneath over-hanging trees, they no longer had the moonlight to help them see.

Suddenly, strong arms swept around her, squeezing the breath from her. 'Had you worried for a minute, didn't I?' Adrian laughed. Then he went silent again as his lips searched for hers.

They lay embracing on the soft grass, locked in the longest kiss Sophie had ever experienced. Her heart was beating so fast she felt it couldn't possibly beat any quicker. It was vibrating her whole body. Then she realized the vibration wasn't caused by her heartbeat. She was trembling. She was scared. She was alone in an unknown country field at night, with a boy she'd known all her life, but whom she suddenly realized she didn't know at all. Not *this* way. She felt completely out of her depth.

She broke off their kiss and struggled out of his arms.

'I — I think I'd like to go now,' she said. She was aware of how prim her voice sounded. She was still shaking.

'Why?' asked Adrian huskily, his arms reaching for her again to pull her back against him.

'*Please!*' she begged desperately. 'Take me home, Adrian.'

'All right.' He staggered to his feet and brushed himself down. 'Come on, then.'

This time he let her climb over the stile first. She led the way back down the lane towards the car, stumbling over tufts of grass, close to tears. He caught her up at the car, zapped the doors open with his remote control, climbed in without a word and started the engine. Sophie fastened her seat-belt and shrank into her seat, her mind struggling to make sense of what had happened.

They drove most of the way home in silence, though when once or twice Sophie did pluck up courage to say something, he sounded perfectly friendly and normal.

'Good night,' he said at the door.

She waited for him to kiss her, but he didn't. He just raised his hand in a signal of farewell and stuck his key in the lock of number twenty-two. She watched him until the door had clicked shut behind him. Only then did she take out her key and let herself in to her own home. She could hear the sound of voices from the lounge. Better say good night, let them know I'm back, she thought, and popped her head around the door.

'Oh, Sophie — hi!' It was her aunt Jill, her father's younger sister. Sophie really liked her but she wasn't in the mood to be sociable right now. She had far too much to think about.

However, if she thought the family would simply let her run off to bed, she was sadly mistaken. She was encouraged to join them. Auntie Jill wanted to know how her exams had gone, while her dad poured her a glass of sherry, which she didn't want and which she swopped for her aunt's much emptier glass when she wasn't looking.

'And how's the boyfriend situation?' Auntie Jill asked merrily. 'I hear there's a romance brewing next door?'

A splutter from Richard saved her. 'S-sorry, a peanut just went down the wrong way,' he apologized.

Sophie shot him a look which said, 'Thanks for rescuing me.'

'He just took me for a spin in his new car, that's all. We're just friends, same as ever,' Sophie said dismissively.

'Oh, what a shame. Still, there's plenty of time for love and you don't want to get too serious, too young,' said Auntie Jill.

'Listen who's talking!' scoffed her dad. His younger sister had got married at eighteen, when she was just two years older than Sophie.

The conversation was switched to a dissection of what went wrong with Auntie Jill's marriage. Sophie got up and yawned loudly and said she hoped they didn't mind if she went to bed.

Once she had closed her bedroom door, she flung herself on her bed, took a deep, shuddering breath and cuddled her teddy-bear. Then she lay still for a while, still clutching her bear. She let her memory carry her back an hour and a half, to when she fell over the stile and landed on top of Adrian. Had he taken that as a signal that she wanted more than just a kiss?

But he hadn't tried to go any further. Why, then, had she felt so scared? It wasn't as if Adrian was a stranger. Why had she trembled like that?

It was that kiss, her instinct told her. She had been so carried away by it that she had almost lost control. For a few

100

seconds, she might have done anything he wanted. She had only just recovered her senses in time. Adrian was older than her. She didn't want to think about how much sexual experience he might have. At nineteen, he was a man, not a boy.

But he'd taken her home when she'd wanted to go. He hadn't objected. He'd been understanding. What did he think of her now? Did he look on her as a mere child? Would he ever ask her out again?

Love's a dangerous thing, she thought, crushing her teddy-bear to her chest and rocking from side to side as if rocking a baby. She dropped a kiss on the old teddy's threadbare head.

'Oh, Teddy, Teddy,' she sighed, feeling tears well up in her eyes and splash down on to the bear's thinning fur. 'What have I done?'

10

Adrian didn't ring the next day. Sophie moped dejectedly round the house. She cheered up as evening approached, figuring he might come round and see her. But the only person to appear from next door was Ian, asking if his mum could borrow the garden shears. He seemed in no hurry to go, and in the end Sophie made him a cup of coffee.

Richard was out, and when Sophie asked where Tara was, Ian said she was out, too. She couldn't bring herself to ask about Adrian. Sophie's father was in the garage and her mother was at her word-processing evening class. Maybe Ian was feeling as lonely as she was, she thought.

He took a thin paperback out of his pocket and passed it to her. 'Have you ever read any of his poems?' he asked.

The book was called *Tourists* and the poet, whose portrait was on the back cover, was a pleasant-looking bearded man called Grevel Lindop. Funny name, thought Sophie. It sounded foreign, perhaps Norwegian.

She flipped through the book and was soon engrossed in a poem called *Buying Valentines*.

'Good, aren't they?' said Ian. 'I love poetry. I write poems, too, you know.'

She stared at him in surprise. 'Do you? I never knew that,' she said.

'I'll show them to you, sometime, if you're interested.' He looked at Sophie, his eyes holding her gaze steadily. A table-lamp was casting its glow on his face and she noticed for the first time that his eyes were hazel, with flecks of gold and green in them, whereas Adrian's eyes were a deep unfathomable brown. Until now, she had always thought Ian's were the same shade.

'Yes, all right,' she agreed. 'I can't write poetry to save my life! In fact, I don't think I've got any talents whatsoever.'

'You must have,' Ian insisted. 'Every-one's got a talent for something. Maybe you just haven't discovered what yours is yet.'

'Maybe you're right.'

All the time they were talking, Sophie kept wishing she could press a button on a remote control and change channels so that Adrian would be sitting there instead of Ian. What was he doing tonight? Did he think he'd upset her and was keeping out of her way? If so, it was up to her to seek him out and tell him everything was all right.

She heard her dad stamping his feet on the backdoor mat, then he walked into the lounge and greeted Ian, who stood up to go, shears in hand.

'See you,' she said. 'Don't forget the poems. Oh, here's your book.'

'Borrow it and give it me back sometime,' he said.

★ ★ ★

The next day was slightly better because Emma, one of her friends from school, came round. They called for Tara and all three of them went off round the shops, had lunch, then went to a movie matinée. Sophie thought how strange it was to be sitting in the cinema with a group of girls instead of with Adrian. At least she was seeing the film! But if only she had been sitting with his arm round her, anticipating another of his kisses . . .

She caught a glimpse of Adrian that evening. As she arrived back with Tara, having seen Emma off on her bus, he was just getting into his car. He waved and drove off.

Pig! thought Sophie. *Beast!* She felt really choked. Why couldn't he at least have said a few words to her?

She realized that Tara was staring at her. She knew what she must be thinking.

'I've been dying to ask you,' Tara said. 'How's it going with Ade?'

Sophie bit her lip. 'Well, we've been out a couple of times so far, but it's no big deal. I'm quite happy to keep it casual,' she lied.

'Look, I'm sorry about what I said to you on the night of the party. I wasn't trying to put you off him,' Tara said. 'I just wanted you to know that he hasn't got a very good track record as far as long relationships are concerned. He goes out with one girl and then another. I . . . I didn't want you to get the wrong idea.'

She stopped. Sophie started at her.

Tara went on: 'I'd love to think of you and Ade going out together. I'd love you both to be happy. Honestly, Sophie!'

Sophie believed her. She smiled. 'Thanks,'

she said. 'So would I. So have a word in his ear and tell him to give me a ring, would you?'

'I'll see what I can do,' promised Tara.

Whether Tara said anything to him or not, Sophie never knew, but, after an interminable Sunday during which he, Ian and Richard all went off somewhere together, he rang on Monday afternoon.

'Hi, there,' he said. 'Fancy doing something tonight?'

'I might,' she replied, trying not to sound too eager.

'I thought you might like to come out for a meal. There's a new Spanish *tapas* bar that's opened in George Street. They've got a flamenco guitarist. Might be fun.'

'Oh, yes, let's go there!' Sophie said enthusiastically.

★ ★ ★

It was hot and crowded in the restaurant and they had to wait at the bar for a table. Sophie wasn't sure what *tapas* meant, but she soon found out when she saw people helping themselves to platefuls of spare ribs, mussels and prawns, bean stews and salads, all arranged in bowls and trays laid on hot-plates.

Tapas was a sort of glorified snacking, she discovered; you had a bit of everything, and most of it was hot and spicy and full of peppers and chilli powder. Weirder than weird were the large black triangular potato crisps which, like everything else, tasted peppery. She gulped down lots and lots of cold mineral water while Adrian drank South American lager.

The guitarist was brilliant. Sophie stopped eating to concentrate on listening and watching the musician's nimble fingers flying over the strings. When she glanced back at Adrian, she was horrified to see a girl standing behind him, her hand on his shoulder. She glared at Sophie, and Sophie, rigid with anger, glared back. Adrian smiled up at the girl, then grinned at Sophie.

'Sophie, this is Mika. Mika — Sophie,' he announced.

The girl with short, glossy black hair ignored Sophie and instead muttered something in Adrian's ear. He laughed and shook his head and the girl went back to the table she had been sitting at, but not before she'd given Sophie another venomous look.

'Who was that?' Sophie asked curtly.

'Oh, just an old girlfriend,' he explained. 'You know what ex's are like, they can be a bit funny sometimes.'

He seemed quite casual and open about the encounter, but it had ruined Sophie's meal. She felt twitchy and couldn't relax, not even when Adrian picked her hand up and kissed it the way he had in the pub.

She was glad to get out of the restaurant and into the fresh air. Adrian had brought the car tonight. He drove home and parked outside the Thompson's house. When he'd switched off the engine, he made no moves to get out. Sophie, who had unfastened her seatbelt and had already opened the passenger door, closed it again.

'Come here,' Adrian said, and put his arm round her.

Sophie felt stiff and unresponsive. The happenings on their previous date still weighed heavily on her mind.

'Adrian,' she ventured, 'I . . . well, I just want to say sorry about the other night.'

'What have you got to be sorry about?' he replied, with laughter in his voice.

'You know. Running away when I did. Making you take me home.'

'That's OK. It was quite late anyway, and I had to get up for work the next morning.'

Sophie felt a great sense of relief and let herself be pulled into his arms. 'Oh, Adrian,' she said. 'It feels so good when we kiss.'

'Sophie, there's something I must ask you,' he said, brushing his lips over her forehead and making her shiver ecstatically. 'Why have you suddenly started to call me Adrian? I've been Ade for years!'

'Because I think it suits you better,' she replied quickly. 'Ade . . . It sounds as though it's short for lemonade, or something. Adrian's got — well, style. It suits your car!'

He burst out laughing. 'Silly girl,' he said, then began to kiss her, and nothing mattered any more, not black-haired girls, or red-hot chillis, or even names.

11

So this was being in love . . . Being totally obsessed with a certain boy; whispering his name last thing at night before sleeping, and first thing in the morning on waking; praying that you'll bump into him; looking in the mirror and seeing if you can smile the way he does, with that special lift of his eyebrow and dimple above the corner of his mouth. And oh, a million more things, like feeling you wanted to keep leaping up and catching leaves, petals, the moon. Laughing to yourself as you remembered things he said. A-dri-an — three perfectly balanced syllables. It was the best name for a boy she had ever heard.

★ ★ ★

She went round to see Tara next day, as soon as she knew Adrian was safely at work.

'We had such a wonderful time last night,' she said breathlessly. 'We went to this *tapas* bar called 'The Cactus' and had all this strange food and there was a guitarist and — '

' 'The Cactus'? Are you sure?' Tara cut in.

'Of course I'm sure! There aren't two Spanish restaurants in a town as small as Caiston, are there? Imagine the proprietors with their holsters and gun belts, fighting it out at noon. 'Hey buddy . . . this place ain't big enough for the both of us.' ' Sophie adopted an exaggerated drawl.

'Are you sure it was Spanish?' Tara asked.

'It had a flamenco guitarist playing Spanish music . . . '

'But it could have been Mexican, right? Tex-Mex, they call that sort of food. Spanish is more tortillas and paellas,' Tara said.

'I . . . I suppose it could have been Mexican, really. There were sombreros and spurs on the wall. Why?'

'Just wondering. I like Spanish food, but not Mexican. If it had been Spanish, I might have been tempted to try it out,' Tara explained.

'You hate curries so you certainly

wouldn't like this,' Sophie informed her. 'I needed about ten bottles of mineral water to cool my mouth down.'

'When are you seeing him again?' Tara asked.

'I don't know. He's got this awful habit of not arranging anything in advance. I mean, most boy-friends would make the next date before they've said good night, but not Adrian. He rings up at the last moment and asks what I'm doing that night.'

'You could always try and pin him down by suggesting a date yourself,' Tara pointed out.

Sophie thought that was probably a good idea and said she would try it out.

★ ★ ★

For the next two evenings, she had things arranged with her female friends, Tara and Janey one night, Emma and Amy another. In the daytime, she hated going out in case she missed a call from him, but if he hadn't phoned by tea-time, she knew she wouldn't be seeing him that night.

On Thursday evening, he came in with Richard shortly after eleven, when Sophie was just going up to bed. She was heartily glad he hadn't left it another fifteen minutes or she would have had her pyjamas on, as well as feeling a fool for going to bed so much earlier than him.

He looked pleased to see her and she quivered inside as his deep gaze swept her from head to foot. 'Doing anything tomorrow night?' he asked.

She shook her head.

'Would you like to come to a party? It's a friend of mine's birthday.'

'Are you going?' she asked Richard.

He shook his head. 'I'm not a friend of Tom's,' he explained.

'I'm sure it wouldn't matter,' Adrian said. 'I'd say I'd invited you.'

'I'd rather not,' insisted Richard.

Sophie looked at her brother critically. He was looking tired, she thought. Must be all the late nights he'd been having beginning to tell. He'd also been trying to fix up a summer job for himself. He'd been making lots of phone calls and had been to see people but hadn't landed anything yet, and as a result he was desperately broke.

She felt sorry for him. How could he possibly take a girl out if he had no money? She knew that their father gave him a bit of pocket-money because she got some, too. But it wasn't enough for more than one visit to the cinema or pub per week. No wonder he didn't want to go to a party. He would have felt mean going along without a few beers or a bottle of wine.

Adrian said he didn't want to take the car as he wanted to be able to enjoy himself. They would go by bus and he would bring her home in a taxi.

'Oh, come on, Richard, you could share our taxi back,' she urged, even though she knew that if he accepted, she would be depriving herself of a chance to cuddle in the cab.

But Richard was adamant that he didn't want to go, so she let the subject drop and arranged to set off with Adrian at nine the next night.

* * *

As soon as Sophie walked through the door of the house where the party was being held, she said anxiously to Adrian, 'I think I'm the youngest person here.'

'I'm sure you're not,' he replied, but to

114

Sophie, all the other guests looked at least Adrian's age and some were a good deal older. One of them she recognized. It was the dark-haired girl from 'The Cactus' restaurant. She was holding hands with a guy in ripped jeans and a surfing T-shirt. She turned her back on Adrian and Sophie and started necking with him.

Adrian asked her what she would like to drink.

'White wine, please,' Sophie said. She felt she needed just one alcoholic drink, even though she hated the taste, in order to give her the courage to stand up to nasty specimens like that girl.

He came back with a brimming paper cup and handed it to her. 'Didn't spill a drop!' he declared triumphantly.

By midnight, Sophie had drunk three cups of wine and was feeling decidedly out of it. There was a rushing noise in her ears and she kept feeling as if she was going to fall over.

'Oops!' she cried, clutching Adrian for support as someone knocked into them.

'Like to dance?' he asked her.

'I don't think I'd better,' she said. 'I'm a bit too drunk.'

'Oh, come on,' he said, pulling her

115

away from the wall she was leaning against.

A fast dance-track was playing. It was the very last thing Sophie should have attempted to dance to as it meant having to move around without anything, or anyone, to hold on to. Still, she bravely tried to make a good, energetic showing, aping the movements of a girl dancing next to her who was hopping from one foot to the other. Next minute, she'd lost her balance and the room and all the people in it were reeling around her.

The next thing she knew she came to, lying on her side on the floor.

'Is she OK?' she heard a girl ask.

'Too much booze,' she heard a male voice reply. Adrian?

Helpful hands pulled her to her feet. 'I'm fine, thanks . . . I'm quite all right,' she heard her voice say, as if from a great distance away. Then she heard someone shrieking with laughter and realized it was herself.

Pull yourself together! she told herself sternly. *Shut up and stop laughing, Sophie. Stand up straight. Look sober!*

Adrian put his arm round her and she just couldn't stop giggling. 'I think I'd better take you home,' he said. 'I'll phone for a taxi.'

It arrived within minutes. As soon as they left the heat and noise behind and were out in the cool night air, Sophie instantly felt ten times drunker. The cab was a blur as she fumbled her way into the back seat. Adrian climbed in beside her.

'I'm sorry, I'm really sorry, I didn't mean to get drunk, I've never been as drunk as this before, I hope you don't think I'm an alco . . . an alco — *hic!* — holic,' she babbled. 'Bloody hiccups,' she cursed.

'An alco-hic-holic? I don't think I've heard of one of those before,' Adrian teased.

'Oh, stop it. It's not fair,' she said crossly. 'It's all right for you, you're sober.'

He put his arm round her and hugged her close. 'I'm not that sober. I've had a few beers,' he said. 'It was that rot-gut wine that did you in. You'll probably have a monster-sized hangover in the morning. Better drink loads of water before you go to bed tonight. It helps stop you getting dehydrated.'

They were silent for a while, during which time Sophie gave up the struggle to focus her eyes on the streets they were driving down and closed them instead. She felt drowsy, almost as if she were dreaming. From somewhere above her head, she heard a voice ask, 'Are you too drunk to kiss me?'

'No,' she whispered.

His lips had never felt more deliciously sexy. She felt as if all her emotions were in the kiss she gave him back. She loved him . . . she loved him.

Obeying her thoughts, her lips formed the words. 'I love you,' she said, hardly aware that the momentous sentence had slipped out.

Although her mind was fuddled, her body was aware of a tension, a drawing back. Suddenly, his arm was no longer around her, his face was no longer close to hers. She struggled to open her eyes.

'We're nearly home,' he said, beginning to search his pockets for his wallet to pay the driver.

But it was a good five minutes before the taxi entered Pevensey Crescent and all that time he remained apart from her, as if they were two polite strangers sharing a cab.

He had to help her out. Her legs started

buckling under her and she realized she felt a bit sick. She handed him her key and he opened the door for her. Then she stumbled up the stairs, hanging heavily on to the banister rail, and just reached the bathroom in time.

★   ★   ★

The next half hour vanished from her memory. She found out the next day that her mother had made her drink a black coffee. She was sick again and then she fell into what could only be described as a drunken stupor before being helped into bed.

When she awoke, she felt dreadful on every count. Pounding headache, sore throat, aching stomach and the most terrible, relentless misery in her heart. She'd let Adrian down. She'd made a fool of the pair of them by getting drunk. Everyone would think now that he had a stupid little girlfriend who couldn't hold her drink.

But even worse than that was her memory of the taxi ride home. *I couldn't have said it,* she thought in panic. *I mustn't have! But I've a horrible feeling I did.*

12

'It's not that bad, Sophie. I'm sure you didn't make a fool of yourself really,' Richard consoled her. She had only told him about getting drunk, not about her dreadful confession in the taxi. She wasn't going to admit that to anybody.

It was four o'clock in the afternoon and she'd only just made it down the stairs. Adrian must have told Tara what had happened because she came round to see how Sophie was, and when all she got was a groan and a 'go away and let me die in peace,' from the other side of the bedroom door, she went away again.

'You weren't there,' Sophie said glumly.

'Look, we've all had a first time for getting drunk,' said Richard. 'I'll never forget mine.' He went on to recount an episode which had taken place on a school trip when he had made himself so ill on draught cider that the coach had had to stop five times for him to be sick on the way home.

'It's different for boys, though. It's part

of being macho. But people don't like it when girls get drunk. There's something disgusting about it,' Sophie said.

'At least you didn't do anything you regret,' he said cheerfully.

'Yes I did!' Sophie said, quickly adding, 'Not that!'

Her bleary eyes registered that there was something different about Richard today. His hair . . .

'You've had your hair cut,' she said. 'It's really nice.'

His loose, shiny blond curls that made him look a bit like a wayward angel had been trimmed and his hair actually had a style for a change. It really suited him.

'Thanks,' he said. 'I had to ask Dad for the money. But something good's come out of it. On the way home I called in at the motor spares place in Gorsey Street and they've offered me a job!'

'Oh, well done!' Sophie cried, then added, 'Ouch! My head! I'd better whisper. *Well done*,' she repeated much more softly. 'When do you start?'

'Monday. I have to be in at eight. You should see the uniform I've got to wear. It's bright orange. I'll look like a carrot in it.'

'A very handsome carrot,' Sophie assured him. She felt so proud of him. Maybe she'd better start looking for a holiday job, too. She certainly needed the money.

'Oh, I feel dreadful,' she moaned.

'A good fry-up's what you need to set you to rights,' announced Mrs Thompson, coming into the lounge with some flowers she'd just picked from the garden.

'Ugh, no way!' said Sophie.

But her mother insisted on producing one and it worked. By six she felt almost healthy again. Certainly, her brain was once more capable of thought — worse luck. She slumped in an arm-chair in front of the television, watching the screen with the sound turned down. She needed to think.

She raised her head and stared at the parting wall. Maybe Adrian was sitting watching telly on the other side. Was he thinking about her? Was he examining his feelings to see if he loved her, too? Oh, why did she have to go and blurt out her feelings like that? And as for her fatal lurch up to the bathroom . . . what a romance killer! She wouldn't blame him if he never wanted to ask her out again.

* ★ ★

By mid-week, it seemed as if Sophie's worst fears were realized. Apart from hearing him drive off to work a couple of times, she hadn't encountered him at all. No visits, no phone calls. Not seeing him, not knowing, was agony. She loved him . . . she missed him. Time after time, her hand reached for the phone to call him at work and suggest they meet, but each time she changed her mind. She couldn't. What if he said 'No'?

By Thursday, she was going frantic. That afternoon, Ian came round to return the garden shears. They sat at the kitchen table with glasses of lemonade and a packet of chocolate digestive biscuits. Sophie remembered his poetry book and gave it back to him.

'You still haven't shown me any of yours,' she rebuked him.

'I'll have to dig some out,' he said. 'Most of them are in a scruffy old notebook. I'll copy one or two out and bring them round.'

'By the way, has Ade been in for the last few nights?' she asked him. 'I was just wondering what he was up to. I haven't seen him for ages.'

She thought her voice sounded casual and normal, but Ian's reaction wasn't normal at all. He looked — and sounded — angry as he replied, 'Makes a change from usual then, doesn't it?'

'What do you mean?' Sophie responded, shocked by the sudden change in his attitude.

'Look, it's none of my business what he gets up to. I'm not his keeper. I haven't seen much of him lately and I haven't a clue where he's been the last few nights. Now, I think I'd better get back. I've got things to do.' Ian snatched up his book and swept out of the house.

How rude! thought Sophie after he'd gone. *And all I did was ask a simple question. Why didn't he simply say, 'He's been out a lot lately.'*

She was doubly angry with Ian. For not only had he been rude, he'd also delivered news she didn't want to hear — that Adrian had been going out in the evenings without her. That surely must mean that it was all over between them. And it was all her own stupid fault!

For the first time ever, she felt she couldn't possibly go round next door, even

124

to see Tara. It was a strange feeling, being excluded from number twenty-two. In the end, she rang Tara, but her mother answered and said she was out. Sophie cried herself to sleep that night.

Next morning, Tara came round looking very bright and happy.

'Guess what? I've got a job!' she shouted at the top of her voice, then flung her arms round Sophie and danced her down the hall.

Sophie was quite envious when she heard that it was in a clothes shop and that Tara would be able to buy things at a discount.

'I can get things for you, too,' Tara promised. 'Just come in and tell me what you want and I'll pretend they're for me.'

It was a lovely sunny morning. Sophie made coffee and they took it out to the garden and sat at the white patio table.

'What's wrong?' Tara asked. 'You've been going round with a face like a wet weekend for days. Has something gone wrong between you and Ade?'

Sophie nodded. 'There was a bit of a disaster on our last date. I would have told you about it but you're never in. Where have you been?'

'Oh, I've been going over to Janey's quite a bit. You know she lives near that sports club? We've been going swimming and we've been playing badminton and things.'

'You didn't invite me!' Sophie protested. She felt quite hurt. Of course Tara had her own friends from school and Sophie had hers, but quite often the two sets mixed and mingled.

A faint flush appeared on Tara's cheeks. 'Sorry,' she said. 'I couldn't, really. A member of the club can only get one non-member in.'

'I see,' Sophie said. 'Oh well . . . you can't have everything. Not even Adrian, it seems. Anyway, your brother took me to this party and . . . '

Sophie told her everything, including the 'I love you' bit which made her blush to recount it.

'Don't worry about it,' Tara said when Sophie had finished her confession. 'I'm sure he was very flattered. I'm sure it gave him an ego the size of a house, if he hasn't got one already.'

'Then why hasn't he asked me out again?' Sophie complained.

'I don't know.' Tara raised her eyes to

heaven. 'Who understands boys? I certainly don't!'

'Nor me,' Sophie said dolefully. 'So you haven't a clue where he's been these last few nights?'

'In all honesty, cross my heart and hope to die — no,' said Tara emphatically.

★ ★ ★

On Saturday night, three of Sophie's friends from school had asked her to go out with them. They were going for a pizza and then on to a club.

At first, Sophie hadn't been keen. She wanted to leave herself free in case Adrian wanted to see her. But when Friday evening came and she still hadn't seen him or heard from him, a very depressed Sophie rang Amy, the girl who was organizing the night out, and asked to be included.

No one can ever tell at the start of an evening exactly how it will end up. Sometimes a long-anticipated party turns out to be the most boring event ever, or a dull and dreaded trip to see a relative turns, by some quirk of fate, into a magical occasion. Sophie went to meet her friends prepared for a reasonable evening with maybe a bit of a dance at the end of it. It wouldn't be a fantastic time because Adrian wasn't there. Though, if he was out with her brother as she suspected, there was always the chance she might bump into him. The town where they lived wasn't that big, after all.

There were four of them — Sophie, Amy, Kirsty and Gemma. They had such fun in the pizza restaurant and laughed so much that they were afraid they might get thrown out. But the waitress smiled tolerantly, glad to see four girls looking and sounding so happy and high-spirited.

'I should come out with you three more often,' Sophie said. 'It's really cheering me up. Much better than sitting at home brooding about Adrian.'

She had told the girls about what had happened and they were all very sympathetic. They realized what a difficult position she was in. If she were to start phoning him at work and going round, it would seem as if she was totally obsessed with him and was chasing him, and it would be guaranteed to frighten him off. In the end, they decided that Sophie should send him a humorous little card, apologizing for getting drunk, and saying she couldn't remember a thing about anything. That way, they could totally ignore the incident and start afresh.

'I'll look for one in the newsagent's tomorrow and put it through his door,' Sophie decided.

'Why don't you bring Tara with you next time we go out? I think she's nice,' Kirsty said.

It had crossed Sophie's mind that she could have invited her — but she was still quite cross with her about being left out of the sports club trips.

Her heart bumped excitedly as they walked up to the entrance to 'Fuzzy's', the club they were to spend the evening in. It was situated just behind the station and the entrance was down some steps at the side of a wine-bar and through a set of heavy, polished wood doors manned by two burly bouncers. They were going early because girls could get in free before ten. She wondered if Adrian and Richard would think of going there tonight. If only . . . She pictured herself in Adrian's arms, dancing close, with him asking her if she'd meant what she'd said in the taxi. She would say she couldn't remember what she'd said and he would remind her. 'You said you loved me. Is it true?'

'Yes,' she would whisper, and he would hold her tightly against him and bring his lips close to hers and murmur, 'I love you, too.' And then he would say how much he wanted to marry her and stay with her for the rest of his life, and he would ask her to get engaged now and marry him when she was eighteen. That was the age at which Auntie Jill got married. Marriage at eighteen ran in the family, so nobody could possibly object. Oh, it was a wonderful, beautiful dream.

They left their jackets at the cloakroom and checked their appearances in the mirror in the ladies loo, then took the plunge into the crowded room where the disco was. Coloured lights were flashing and there were loads of boys standing round the bar.

Kirsty spotted Darren Hale from their school and went up to talk to him. The others knew that she fancied him, so they kept away in order to give her a chance to chat him up.

'Here's your Coke.' Amy thrust a damp, cold glass into Sophie's hand. It was very hot in the club so she gratefully took a lengthy swig.

'Excuse me, would you like to dance?'

Sophie looked up in surprise. The boy who was inviting her, in such correct, stilted English, wore white jeans and a brightly-coloured baggy shirt. He had fair hair and a nice smile, but wasn't a patch on Adrian. Still, she decided to accept because, if Adrian *was* there, making him jealous might not be such a bad thing!

'Watch my drink for me,' she asked Gemma, who was so busy talking to Amy that no boy would have got a word in edgeways.

They found a space in the throng and started to dance.

'I am called Janek. I come from Poland,' the boy told her, fighting to make himself heard above the loud, thumping beat. 'I am a student at St Christopher's College. I am learning English.'

Sophie introduced herself but it was impossible to talk much because of the volume of the disco. One dance followed another, but when it got to a third and the track seemed to be going on and on, Sophie feigned exhaustion and went back to where Amy and Gemma were. The ice in her drink had long since melted and it was now lukewarm, but it tasted heavenly to the thirsty Sophie.

'Please . . . may I?' Janek held out his hand towards Sophie's glass and, taken aback, she let him take it. When he handed it back without an apology, there was hardly a drop left.

'Make him get you another,' muttered Amy, giving Sophie a nudge.

Sophie turned back, intending to follow Amy's advice and found, to her surprise, that he was walking away, without even saying, 'Thanks', or 'Goodbye'.

'What a cheek!' she exclaimed to Amy.

Gemma thought it was funny. 'He probably makes a habit of it, asking girls to dance then stealing their drink. That way, he can keep drinking all night for free.'

'Huh! And I thought it was my pretty face he was after,' complained Sophie jokingly. In truth, she didn't really care. There was only one boy with whom she wanted to dance and he wasn't there.

Another boy asked her to dance. He was very good-looking and so Sophie accepted. It was impossible to talk over the noise of the music, so they just grinned at each other — and it was during one of these grins that Sophie saw him, over her partner's shoulder. Adrian ... dancing with that horrible girl with the short black hair! Sophie's feet stopped dancing and she stood frozen to the spot. As she watched, Adrian pulled the girl into his arms and started kissing her.

Sophie felt sick. 'Excuse me,' she muttered and dashed away from her partner and off the dance floor. Amy and Gemma were still talking by the bar. Sophie grabbed Gemma's sleeve and collapsed on to the edge of the table.

'Come on, we've got to get out of here!' she cried wildly. 'Where's my coat? I've got to go!'

'Calm down! Tell us what's happened,' Amy said.

Sophie told them.

'The best thing you could do is to let him see you dancing with another boy as if you didn't have a care in the world,' Gemma said.

'I *was* dancing with another boy, but I don't think he saw me,' wailed Sophie. 'And anyway, I *do* care! I want to go home.'

Amy and Gemma looked at each other.

'I'll go and tell Kirsty. I think she wants to stay here with Darren,' Amy said.

'I don't want to spoil your evening. I'm quite all right on my own,' Sophie promised.

'At least let us see you on to the bus,' Gemma said.

'Then you won't be able to get back into the club,' Sophie pointed out. 'Look, I'll go. I'll be OK. I'll ring you tomorrow, let you know I got back safely.'

The others reluctantly agreed. When Sophie pushed her way against the tide of people coming into the club, and emerged at the top of the steps, she found herself gasping. She felt quite shaky. It had been terrible, seeing Adrian with that girl. As she walked down the road towards the bus terminus, she thought about it, and the more she thought, the angrier she got. He had been using her, that much was clear. So much for that girl being an ex! Their relationship was still very much alive. They'd had some temporary split-up and he wanted to be seen around with someone else to make his real girlfriend jealous. She, Sophie, had fitted the bill perfectly!

I wonder if Tara knew about the girl?

wondered Sophie as she headed for her bus-stop. No, she couldn't have, Sophie decided. She would have warned her. Then Sophie remembered that, in the beginning, Tara *had* tried to warn her off Adrian. Then she'd had a mysterious change of heart and started encouraging their relationship. Strange, that . . .

She was just in time to see a bus pulling away from the stop. Drat! That meant a twenty minute wait until the next one. She felt so upset and forlorn that she almost burst into tears in public, but just about managed to pull herself together. Tears could wait until she was alone.

She wasn't prepared to stand in the street all that time. There was a small greasy-spoon café just down the road. She would go in there and have a coffee to pass the time.

One coffee wasn't enough to soothe her shattered nerves and she had to order another. She sipped it too soon after it was made and winced as the scalding liquid touched her lips. The burning feeling reminded her of Adrian's kisses. Those false, meaningless kisses. Oh, thank heavens she hadn't lingered in that country field with him. Just imagine if she'd . . . No, it didn't bear thinking about. She'd had a lucky escape and she never wanted to see him again. *Or* his brother. Oh, why did they have to live next door? It wasn't fair!

It's my fault, though, she reminded herself. If she hadn't gone and developed that fancy for him after the Framlingham trip, everything would have remained exactly as it had always been between the Thompsons and the Cassells — good, reliable, trustworthy friends. Now that friendship was turned to dust, littered with broken hearts, she thought dramatically.

A glance at her watch told her that her bus was due to leave in five minutes. Leaping up, she felt for her purse in her bag. It wasn't there. Cold terror crept over her. It *had* to be there! She felt for it again. She tried her pockets . . . No purse. Oh God, what was she going to do? No purse didn't only mean no money for the coffees, it also meant no bus fare home!

13

Sophie trembled as she approached the woman at the till.

'I . . . I seem to have lost my purse,' she said, willing the woman to believe her.

Her words were received with an icy stare from narrowed eyes. 'You'll have to think up something better than that,' she snapped. 'I must hear that one every day from school-kids trying to get something for nothing.'

'But I'm *not* trying to get something for nothing!' Sophie insisted, sure that her genuine distress must be quite obvious to anybody. 'I have really, seriously lost my purse and now I don't know . . . how I'm g-going to get home.' Her voice broke into a sob and suddenly she was overwhelmed by tears as the shock of seeing Adrian and that girl together, coupled with the shock of losing her purse, got too much for her.

She pulled a tissue out of her bag and started to mop her eyes.

'You'll win an Oscar for it, love,' said the disbelieving woman sarcastically.

'I'm going to m-miss my last bus home,' Sophie wailed. 'It's going any minute now.'

'If you leave here without paying for those coffees, I'm going to call the police,' said the woman harshly.

'Here you are.' There was the rattle of coins landing on the glass counter. 'Come on, Sophie, run — we'll just make it.'

Her arm was grabbed and she was flying towards the bus-stop before it registered just who her rescuer was. '*Ian!*' she gasped. 'What — '

'Ssh. Keep running. We can talk on the bus.'

The driver had just closed the doors when they arrived. Ian rapped on them and the driver opened them again and glared at the pair of them. 'You're very lucky,' he said grumpily. 'Try not to cut it so fine next time.'

It was a double-decker and they went upstairs and found a seat together. It took Sophie some seconds to get her breath, and when she did, she gazed wide-eyed at Ian, thinking that he was like a legendary knight who had arrived on his white horse and saved the princess from the jaws of death. Well, the police at any rate!

'I don't know how I can ever thank you,'

she said. 'How come . . . I mean . . . ?' Her words tailed off but Ian knew what she was trying to say.

'I'd spent the evening with some friends. I was walking past the café on my way to catch the bus myself and I just happened to glance in and there you were, crying your eyes out. I knew something had to be wrong, so I came in.'

'But you might have missed the bus!' she pointed out.

'Then there would have been two of us to share a taxi. Why couldn't you pay your bill?' he asked.

Sophie told him how she and her friends had gone to 'Fuzzy's' and how she reckoned someone had stolen her purse when she'd put her bag down by the table while she was dancing with the crazy Pole. 'Emma and Amy were there, but they were jawing away. I reckon someone just dipped their hand in and took it and they didn't notice.'

'Did you have much money in it?' Ian asked her.

'Only about a fiver. It's no great tragedy.'

'It might have been if I hadn't come past when I did . . .'

'Oh, Ian . . . ' Her mind shot back to how they had parted the other day, how rude and snappy he'd been. Well, she was prepared to forgive him now. So — she was on good terms with Tara and Ian; two out of three. But would she ever be able to forgive the third?

Just then Ian smiled and a pang shot through her as she realized, for the first time, how similar to Adrian's his smile was. His eyelashes were longer than Adrian's and his greeny-brown eyes sparkled through them. His hair shone like burnished copper under the bus's interior lights. He looks like a poet, she thought.

On an impulse, she said, 'You said you were going to dig out some of your poems for me.'

'I've got my notebook on me, if you think you can read my writing. Hang on . . . '

He dug the battered object out of the inside pocket of his grey jacket and started leafing through it. 'Some of them are old ones, they're not very good. Let's see . . . '

Sophie tried hard to read some of the words as he flipped through the book. Now, there's this one that might be appropriate. It's called *The Tear*.'

140

He handed the notebook over. It was a very short poem and he had written it out so that the shape of the poem itself resembled a teardrop:

now
in a heart
by necessity hardened
an outcrop of rock crystal
rough, brilliant, cold and beautiful
is chiselled by a sharp grief
and molten, wells upwards
where it dazzles the
world with
wonder
why

Sophie didn't know quite what to make of it. 'It's a bit sort of experimental, isn't it?' she said. 'Are all your poems like this?'

Ian shook his head. 'No, that was a one-off. I was trying to copy a style known as 'concrete poetry'. Most of my others are more normal.'

'Can I see another one?' she asked.

'Did you mean it when you said you were with your friends tonight?' Ian asked.

'Of course!' Sophie declared, her eyes wide with surprise. 'Why should I lie?'

'Just checking,' he replied mysteriously.

Sophie furrowed her brow. Ian was so unpredictable, she thought. She honestly never knew what he was going to say or do next. If only she didn't have such a painful ache in her heart with the name 'Adrian' attached to it, she might seek out lots more interesting conversations with him. Ian was getting better the older he got, she reflected. He'd been a quiet, shy kid, always with his nose in a book, but it had paid off. She had a feeling he was going somewhere.

They were nearing their stop. Sophie began to rise from her seat but Ian was blocking her way. He was tearing a page out of his note-book. Sophie rang the bell just in time and they lurched downstairs as the bus braked rather sharply.

'Make your minds up a bit sooner next time,' said the grumpy driver.

The moment they had alighted, Sophie burst out laughing. Then she wondered how it was she could laugh when her heart was supposed to be breaking. Adrian . . .

They reached Sophie's door. Fortunately, her keys hadn't been in the missing purse.

'Thanks again,' she said. 'I must make it

up to you somehow.'

'Perhaps you'll think of a way after you've read this,' Ian said, holding out the folded sheet of paper from his notebook. 'Read it when you're on your own.'

His tone was quiet, his eyes penetrating and serious as he stared at her, solemn-faced. A hush seemed to have descended on the whole street as Sophie took the piece of paper from him.

'Good night,' he said and turned into his own gate, leaving Sophie staring after him, feeling that the world had suddenly gone crazy around her.

14

Sophie was still staring bemusedly at the door to Ian's house when a pair of strong arms threw themselves round her from behind and squeezed her. She opened her mouth to scream, then closed it when she recognized a familiar laugh.

'Richard! How could you? You nearly gave me a heart attack!'

'Don't think I'm prying, but wasn't that Ian I saw you with, not Adrian? You're not two-timing, are you?'

'If I was, I'd have more sense than to do it so close to home,' she pointed out. 'Oh, Richard, I've had such a terrible night. I lost my purse and Ian rescued me and — '

'Ssh,' Richard said. 'You're raising your voice. You'll wake the whole street up and it's twenty-to-one. Tell me indoors.'

They went in.

'I fancy a mug of hot chocolate. How about you?' said Richard.

The idea sounded blissful to Sophie.

'I'll make it,' he said. 'You sit down. Sounds like you've had a tough time.'

144

'You've no idea how tough,' she sighed, collapsing on to a kitchen chair. As the kitchen was in an extension, they could talk there without fear of waking their parents.

Shall I or shan't I tell him about Adrian? she wondered as he was making the hot chocolate. Did he have any idea what was going on? He was closer to Adrian than anybody else, even Tara. If anyone knew the situation with that dark-haired girl, Richard would.

When they were both sitting down with their mugs, Sophie decided to risk it. 'I went to 'Fuzzy's' with Amy and Co. Adrian was there with a girl.' She waited for Richard's reaction.

'What did she look like?' he asked.

'Black hair, Mediterranean-looking. White cropped top and jeans.' She then told him about encountering the same girl in 'The Cactus'.

'Oh, dear,' Richard sighed gustily. 'Sounds like Mika's back on the scene. Oh, Sophe, I am sorry. I know how you must feel. But at least it's Mika, not some stranger he's just picked up.'

Every word her brother spoke clanged like a bell of doom. There was such a tone

145

of finality in his voice. 'Who's Mika?' she asked almost in a whisper.

'The love of Ade's life, if he can be said to have one. No disrespect to you, Sophie, but he was madly in love with her about six months ago. She's Israeli and she works as an *au pair* for a family in Fallowfield. She and Ade had a major row because he found out she'd gone out with someone else one night. They split up. Then she went back home for a visit, and she came back just after he asked you out,' Richard explained.

'I had a nasty feeling that he was desperately looking for a new girlfriend just because he was on the rebound,' continued Richard. 'When he told me he was taking you out, I told him what I'd do to him if he messed my sister around. He assured me he wouldn't, that he genuinely wanted to go out with you, and I wished him luck. But it looks like you got caught up in his complicated love life. I did try to warn you, Sophe.'

'I know you did. It all makes perfect sense, doesn't it? I'd kind of figured it out for myself already,' she said dolefully.

'I'm going to punch him in the face tomorrow for this,' Richard said fiercely.

'Don't bother. I'm perfectly capable of punching him myself. But I don't see why I should waste my energy or the appearance of my knuckles,' Sophie said, equally angrily. 'He's a — ' She called him a few choice names. 'To think I've got to carry on living next door to him after this!'

'There's only one cure for a broken heart and that's to find someone else as quickly as possible,' Richard said.

'Is that what *you* do?'

'I haven't had to put it to the test yet. I haven't got emotionally involved enough with anybody to get my heart broken. But you never know, it could happen,' he said with a shrug, and went back to sipping his hot chocolate. 'Well, I think I'll take this up to bed with me. Good night, Sis, try not to take it too hard. Plenty of other fish in the sea, and all that.'

'Plenty of other rats in the garbage can,' she muttered in response. 'Good night.'

She thought that once she was alone in her room, she'd cry her eyes out, but she didn't. She was so physically and emotionally exhausted that she fell asleep straight away.

★ ★ ★

147

It wasn't until the morning that she remembered the poem that Ian had given her . . .

'*Read it when you're on your own . . .*' Sophie could hear Ian's voice echoing in her mind. What on earth was in it that meant she couldn't read it with anyone else around? Would she burst out laughing? Crying? Would the words make her want to beat somebody up? Rob a bank? Take her money and go off round the world? Surely poetry couldn't affect you that much?

She took the folded, ruled page out of the pocket of the denim jacket she'd been wearing the previous evening. As soon as she saw the title, she knew exactly why Ian had asked her to make sure she was on her own.

15

ODE TO SOPHIE THOMPSON

Sophie. Rhymes with tree, rhymes
   with free,
If only Sophie T. would rhyme with
   me.
Beautiful Sophie with her untamed
   hair
And eyes like a forest's cool green
   lair,
So many times I've watched and
   hoped and wept,
Pined at her window wondering if
   she slept.

I wonder if she ever thinks at all
Of kids who once had bucket, spade
   and ball
And screamed and played in seas of
   indigo
On sultry August days so long ago?
Oh, Sophie, I can see you now. Pink
   top,

On which ice-cream would somehow
   always drop,
Blue shorts, white hat on that cas-
   cade of curls —
No wonder I can't look at other
   girls.
My heart's a beach, a peach still on
   the tree,
A flash of green, a summer memory
Of love both then and now for
   Sophie T.

Sophie's first reaction on getting to the
end of it was, oh, no! What a terrible,
ghastly coincidence! She was in love with
Adrian and Ian was in love with her. What
was she going to do now?

Nobody had ever told her they loved her
before. And he'd put it down on paper,
too! Despite her consternation, a funny,
warm, delighted feeling was rising up
inside her. Her first ever love-poem!

She read it again more slowly. Ice-cream
on her top, indeed! Had she really been
such a messy child, or had he only put that
bit in to help the rhyme?

I must have been really blind, she told
herself. *Did he really pine at my
window, like I pined looking out of*

mine for Adrian?

She recalled his visit to return the garden shears. No wonder he'd got so annoyed when she asked about Adrian. He was jealous — and worried. He'd probably known about Mika all along. And to think of her kissing Adrian at the party, right in front of Ian! Ian had probably hoped that, by being even friendlier now, he would be the one she'd turn to once Adrian had let her down, as he inevitably would.

She read the poem for a third time and felt warm and melty inside. Adrian might not care about her, but someone did. It was such a lovely poem. But how was Ian expecting her to react? Surely he didn't think she could fall straight from Adrian's arms into his?

What do I feel about Adrian now? she asked herself. Let down; angry; hurt; insulted. They were the words that rang true. Love? No. No way. He'd killed it stone dead. Adrian Cassell was nothing but a handsome face. So much for knights of old! Any chivalrous knight would have run someone like Adrian through with his lance for insulting a lady.

A little dagger twisted in her heart, though, when she thought about that face close to hers, and his lips kissing hers. It would take a while for the pain to go away. It wouldn't wear off in a few hours, or a few days. Ian had better not hassle her, she couldn't stand it. If he had any sensitivity, he'd keep his distance for a while.

Did Adrian see me in 'Fuzzy's'? That was the burning question. If he hadn't seen Sophie there, then he would have no idea that she was so hurt and furious. What was she going to do? And what about poor Ian? She knew only too well what it felt like to be in love with someone who didn't appear to return the same feelings.

What did she think of Ian? Really, truly? She recalled their bus journey home the previous night, when she'd thought how nice-looking he was. She'd never noticed him in that way before. She'd always thought of him as a gawky lad. He had gorgeous hair and stunning eyes. He'd grown taller and filled out, too. In fact, when she thought about it, Adrian was a weeny bit weedy. Ian had muscles.

Her heart gave a sudden bump and she reached for the poem again. It wasn't just a 'roses are red, violets are blue' type of verse, it had some real thought in it. Were her eyes the same shade of green as a forest? Did he mean a coniferous one or a deciduous one? Not that it mattered. What mattered was that he had noticed her eyes and thought about them. She couldn't imagine Adrian doing that. The only things he saw any poetry in were the lines of a car and the sound of its engine. Cars, not girls, were the real passion in his life.

Ian was more like her — thoughtful, with deep feelings. She could imagine walking in the country with him, enjoying looking at wildlife and beautiful scenery. He appreciated things like that, as she did. Oh, they could share so much!

I shouldn't be thinking like this, she told herself. Not so soon after Adrian. But, strangely, the power of Adrian was fading. It was being replaced by something much more exciting. How could she have known Ian all these years and not realized his qualities? *In the same way as I knew Adrian all those years and suddenly found him attractive*, she reminded herself ruefully. Time wrought changes. In people, in feelings, in the things that happened every day. *I'll be writing a poem in a minute if I carry on being so reflective*, she thought wryly. *That would impress Ian!*

It struck her, with a shock, that she *did* want to impress Ian; that she liked him a lot, that he intrigued her, that she'd like to get closer to him. A whole lot closer . . .

★ ★ ★

At a quarter-past-two she was just putting down her spoon after polishing off a strawberry yoghurt when there was a rap at the back door and a male voice called out, 'Hello, Sophie — are you there?'

Sophie froze. She couldn't tell if it was Adrian or Ian as their voices were quite similar. She prepared to make a dash away from the door, to go and hide. She was about to tell her mother to say she wasn't in when whoever it was opened the back door and came in. It was Ian, thank goodness!

She greeted him with a wide, welcoming smile. 'I've got some money for you, to pay you back for last night. Hang on, I'll just go and get it.'

She ran upstairs to her room and came back with two pound coins. Ian put out his hand to take them and as she dropped them into his palm their fingers touched and an electric shock sizzled right up

154

Sophie's arm. It was such a powerful feeling that her mouth dropped open and she couldn't say a word. Had Ian felt it, too? He didn't say anything either, just looked at her with that steady, soul-searching gaze of his.

Help, she thought, I think I've just fallen in love!

16

Sophie felt breathless, fluttery, as light and drifty as a butterfly. If the slightest wisp of a breeze had caught her, she would have wafted away, out of the window, over the tree-tops, above the houses, into the sky, higher and higher. That was how she felt.

Ian's eyes held hers, as if by the sheer force of his look he was pinning her to the earth, keeping her from floating away. She had to say or do something to break the tension. Her mother was crashing crockery in the sink. There was too much noise to concentrate.

'Let's go in the garden,' she said.

She led the way and Ian followed. It was a damp, breezy day and Sophie was wearing a short-sleeved T-shirt. She rubbed her arms to keep warm.

'I read the poem. It was . . . ' While she struggled to supply the right adjective, a kind of nervous twitch flicked across his face. She knew she was keeping him in suspense and it was dreadful of her.

'Did you like it?' he asked. 'Did you

mind my giving it to you? Would you rather I'd kept it to myself and not told you?'

He smelled wonderful, she noticed. He had on a fragrance that was much nicer than either of the ones Adrian used. And he looked fantastic. Strong and solid and so good-looking.

'I'm glad you gave it to me. It was really good. Brilliant, in fact,' she said, aware of how lame her words sounded.

He looked relieved. 'I thought you might be angry,' he said.

'I think you were very brave giving it to me,' she said.

'Yes, I thought so, too,' he replied, with a little laugh and his eyes brightened. 'Especially when I know how you feel about Ade,' he added. The light died in his eyes and they went bleak and shadowy.

'Oh, *him*,' Sophie said heavily.

'I know you're in love with him and I knew I was probably making a fool of myself, giving you the poem, but I thought it was time to be honest,' he said. 'I'm not like my brother. I couldn't do what he does, picking up girls and dropping them, playing one against the other like he did with you. I'm going to tell you something.

It might sound like sour grapes on my part, but it's something I think you ought to know . . . '

Sophie stiffened. She felt her heartbeat quicken and her fingers began to curl and clench. She didn't want to hear what Ian was going to say. She knew she wouldn't like it one bit. She felt as if she'd just climbed into the chair at the dentist's as she steeled herself for the emotional onslaught of his words.

'Right from the start, even before Mika came back, he was playing a game with you, Sophie. Do you know what he said? He said, 'Sophie's so sweet and naive. I'm going to see how long it takes to get her to fall in love with me. Three dates and a few mysterious absences and I'll have the kid eating out of my hand'.'

Ian swung his foot and lightly kicked a green plastic watering can that was standing next to the wall, then turned his eyes back to Sophie. They were a blazing, incandescent glitter. 'How do you think I felt, feeling the way I do about you and hearing him say that? I could have punched his face in!' he raged. 'But all I said was, 'Sophie's our neighbour, you can't treat her like that'. If I'd have said any more, he would have made my life a misery.'

He let his angry breath out in a great, 'Huh!' and strode away across the garden. When he got to the shed he turned back, raised a hand and swept his hair back from his brow. The poet look again, thought Sophie.

'I'm sorry. I always seem to be losing my temper in front of you,' he said, managing a half grin.

'It's all right. I understand,' Sophie murmured.

'When your most powerful feelings are involved . . . well, you know.'

'Yes, I do,' Sophie agreed. She was waiting with bated breath for Ian to really declare himself; for him to say he wanted her to forget his brother and make a go of it with him.

But he didn't. Instead, a sad, wistful look moved over his expressive face and he said, 'It's all right. I won't bother you any more. I know now that you can never feel anything special for me. I just hope this hasn't spoiled our friendship and that we can go on the way we always have. You can keep the poem. Bye.'

And he was off, kicking open the gate

between the gardens.

'But — ' Sophie's mouth opened and closed. 'Ian, come back!' she called. But it was too late. The back door of number twenty-two had slammed firmly shut.

★ ★ ★

If there was to be a show-down with Adrian, it was a long time coming. The fact that he hadn't phoned or been round seemed to indicate either that he knew she'd seen him in the club, or that he'd dropped her in the cruellest way, without a word of apology or explanation. Sophie was reminded of the fiasco of their very first date, when he'd let Richard lure him to the pub and hadn't had the grace to phone her. She was well out of it, she reflected. Just imagine if she'd been going steady with him, or engaged to him — or even married! It would be terrible, she'd never be able to trust him an inch.

She kept Ian's poem under her pillow, until it began to look a bit squashed. Then she copied it out and kept it between the pages of her diary and put the original in a shoe-box full of keepsakes in her dressing-table drawer.

Ian's love for her was over, too, of course. Over before it had had a chance to begin. Whilst she had been going through a cooling-off period towards Adrian, Ian, on his side of the wall, must have been cooling off towards her. He'd certainly been keeping out of her way, like he'd said he would.

She hadn't seen him in the garden, or outside the house, since that day when they'd talked about his poem. It was dreadful. She wanted to see him so much. She still got that strange, dizzy, floaty feeling whenever she thought about him, or read his poem.

Oh, Ian, she sighed out loud. What she felt for him was so different to what she'd felt for Adrian; so much more real, somehow. And, for a short while, he had been there for her, ready to fall in love but she had missed it. It was tragic. Positively Shakespearian.

Also — and this was very strange, considering how close they had always been — she hadn't seen much of Tara. She'd bumped into her once as she was flying out of the house.

'Just off to Janey's. See you!' she'd yelled, and had dashed up the road towards the bus-stop, red hair bouncing on her shoulders. Sophie wondered if Tara had put a slight, temporary distance between them because of Adrian. Perhaps she was being tactful.

Sophie started seeing more of her friends from school, Kirsty, who had been going out with Darren ever since that fateful night at 'Fuzzy's', and Gemma and Amy. After Sophie had left that night, Gemma had been chatted up by a bloke who turned out to be a fireman. She'd gone out with him once but said it was a matter of 'all hands to the pump' and so she'd finished with him!

'We must go out on a man-hunt one night soon,' Amy said.

'Count me in!' clamoured Gemma.

Sophie was reluctant, thinking of what happened last time, but in the end she went. Not to 'Fuzzy's', though. A new club had opened called 'Chasm'. They went there one night and Sophie danced the others under the table. Her feet just wouldn't stop. It was as if she was dancing the past right out of her system. One by one, Gemma, Kirsty and Amy dropped out until Sophie was dancing alone. She revelled in the movements of her body.

She felt strong and invincible. I'm free, she thought. I don't need anybody.

When she finally gave in to exhaustion and dropped into her seat at their table, depression set in to replace her earlier elation. There was a difference between need and want, she realized. Maybe she didn't need anybody, but she did want Ian. The more absent he made himself, the more fascinated she became. There was so much potential there and they were wasting time. The holidays were slowly ticking away.

They were all waiting in trepidation for their exam results. They all expected to go on into the Sixth Form. Leaving school was an unthinkable prospect as none of them had a clue what they wanted to do.

Richard was still going out regularly three or four evenings a week. Sophie marvelled at the fact that he wasn't brooding about his results, even though they were even more crucial than hers. He seemed to be taking an undue interest in his appearance. Sophie knew he had to be seeing a girl, not just going out with the lads, because before each departure there would be much ironing of shirts followed by a long, hot shower, a mammoth hair-combing and gelling session, and he would finally come down the stairs in a miasma of cologne which always set her mum coughing and spluttering.

'Really, Richard, do you have to use so much? Hasn't your girlfriend got a sense of smell?' their mum enquired, holding her nose.

Richard would just smile and drift out of the door, leaving them all wondering. They would hear his motorbike (now mended) revving up, then he'd be off in a huge roar and a scattering of small pebbles. Yet he was always back quite early. There were no more of his two or three o'clock in the morning returns, where he'd make such an effort not to wake anyone up that he'd bump into something and wake them all up anyway. Now, he was always back before one o'clock.

Once, Sophie tackled him head on. It was Saturday afternoon and he was doing some weeding in the garden.

'How's the job going?' Sophie enquired, working up subtly to the big question.

'Oh, not bad. I told you the other day about Kevin being off because his dad had died?'

Sophie nodded. 'Well, he's decided not

to come back. He's moving into his mother's house over in Granton and he's taking over his father's old business. So guess who's been promoted? I'm getting more money now and it almost makes it worthwhile getting out of bed in the morning!'

'That's great,' Sophie said. 'I don't see nearly enough of you these days. What are you up to? I've never seen you making so much effort with your appearance, just to go out for the evening. What's her name?'

'Oh, it's nobody. I haven't got a girlfriend. But one can always hope, ha-ha!' Richard must have tried very hard to control himself, because the colour in his face came and went, and finally got the better of him, suffusing his cheeks with crimson so that he looked utterly guilty of something. But what?

Then, one evening shortly after that, Sophie found out exactly what it was.

17

The police thriller she had been watching had come to an end. Sophie flipped through the channels but there was nothing interesting on. It was just before midnight when she switched off. She was a bit sleepy and she decided to make a cup of hot chocolate and take it up to bed. The armchair she was in was really comfy. She didn't feel like moving. The room was so silent that she sat there against the cushions, relishing the peace.

She was alone in the house but it didn't occur to her to feel scared. Nothing ever happened in Pevensey Crescent. They had a Neighbourhood Watch scheme and there hadn't been a burglary for ages, thank goodness.

It was so very quiet in the lounge that she could hear the ticking of the electric clock on the wall. Then, all of a sudden, she heard something else, something that made her tense up and set all the little hairs down her arms and up the back of her neck prickling with apprehension. It was a kind of scuffling sound and it came from outside the front window.

Cats! she thought, scornful of her fear. Then she heard it again, and this time it wasn't just a scuffling noise, there was a sort of moaning sound with it as well!

Terror washed over her, making her weak and faint. What should she do? Should she dial 999 and get the police? But what if she did that and it *was* only an animal? An animal in pain, perhaps . . . a dog that had been hit by a car. Or a fox. She knew foxes had been glimpsed in back gardens nearby. They lived in the park and in the wild land bordering the railway line. Perhaps it was the RSPCA she should be ringing, not the police.

There it was again! Without thinking twice, Sophie leaped to her feet, switched off the light, then peeked round the edge of the curtains. She couldn't see anything in the front garden and she was about to retreat, puzzled, when suddenly something moved. Or rather, loomed. A great, dark, dense shape came lurching right towards where she stood at the window.

With a shriek of fear, Sophie bolted from the window. She stood quaking in the middle of the room, listening. Silence

. . . then, unmistakably, the sound of human voices. A male one, then a female one, giggling a response.

Huh! she thought furiously. *So much for injured animals or burglars. It's my blasted brother and the girlfriend he won't tell me about. Well, I'll teach them to scare me half to death!*

She strode purposefully into the kitchen, seized a saucepan off the shelf and filled it with cold water. This, she carried upstairs, a triumphant grin on her face. *I'll really get that brother of mine this time,* she crowed to herself as, smiling broadly, she silently pushed open the heavy double-glazed window in her parents' bedroom. In the gloom, she located the tops of two heads in the corner between the porch and the front wall and, with a cry of, 'Gotcha!' she emptied the contents of the pan over them.

The screams that greeted her ears must have woken the whole street. But her glee was cut short when she saw whose faces were turned up to hers, woeful and dripping. One, sure enough, belonged to her brother. But it was the identity of the girl he had been kissing that caused Sophie the greatest shock. It was none other than Tara!

★ ★ ★

Shocked, hurt, upset, left out, let down, cheated . . . all these words and more described how Sophie felt. She had been doubly lied to, both by her brother and by Tara. So Richard had no girlfriend? Pull the other one! And Tara was spending all her time at the sports club with Janey? Like hell she was!

She fumed for hours before falling asleep.

In the morning, Richard was tactfully absent. According to their father, he had gone for a ride on his bike. She waited to see if Tara would call round and explain, thinking she probably wouldn't have the courage. However, shortly after eleven, Tara appeared and, to Sophie's amazement, seemed to think the discovery and the drenching was all very funny!

'I might have known my sins would find me out in the end,' she said merrily. 'Talk about dampening the flames of ardour!'

'Why didn't you tell me?' demanded Sophie furiously, as soon as she'd got Tara up to her room. 'You're supposed to be my friend, for heaven's sake! Though you haven't been much of one lately. I've hardly seen you, and I could have done with some help and advice after the way your brother's treated me.'

Tara gave a sheepish grimace. She kicked off her blue espadrilles, sat down cross-legged on the floor and stared at her lap.

'Did you think I'd disapprove?' Sophie asked.

'Well . . . ' said Tara.

'Oh, come on,' said Sophie crossly. 'You're supposed to be my friend! How long has this been going on?'

'Weeks,' Tara said, looking sheepish.

'So that story about Janey and the sports club?'

'It was true!' Tara countered hotly. 'I've been there quite a few times. As soon as Richard got his job, I was at a loose end in the daytimes, but if I'd gone places with you, you'd have wanted to know what I was doing in the evening, and how could I tell you I was going out with Richard?'

'Easily,' Sophie snorted. 'What's wrong with it? And why did Richard think he had to hide it from me? I don't understand you two.'

'Think about it,' Tara said. 'You'd started going out with my horrible brother. Richard and I both knew the truth about him and tried to warn you in the gentlest ways we could, but we knew you were too besotted to listen. I've fancied your brother for ages but I didn't think I stood a chance until that day you told me he was worried about getting involved with anyone in case it broke up when he went off to university. That meant he didn't have anybody and I was in with a chance.'

Sophie carried on listening, open-mouthed.

'Remember when you came up to my bedroom at the party and I said I had something in my eye?' continued Tara. 'That was a lie. I'd been crying my eyes out because Richard was chatting-up that awful Carol-Ann.'

'I thought it seemed a bit suspicious at the time. *Both* your eyes looked red,' said Sophie.

'Remember ages ago when I asked you if you fancied Ade?'

Sophie nodded.

'At the time, I thought it would be great

if we could all start double-dating. I thought it would be really neat if we both fell in love with each other's brothers. But you said you didn't fancy him.'

'That was a lie,' said Sophie.

'I think we've both told a few,' Tara said ruefully.

For some reason, Sophie suddenly remembered the night Auntie Jill had referred to romances next door and Richard had had a choking fit. That explained that! It had been guilt, not a peanut he'd been choking on.

A silence fell between them, during which Sophie reflected that she didn't know where she stood with anybody at the moment, or how she felt about them. 'I still don't understand why you felt you couldn't tell me. It's really hurtful,' she said.

Tara looked Sophie straight in the eye. 'How could I throw my happiness in your face?' she said. 'If you and Ade had been happy together, I'd have told you. But seeing everything going wrong, and you so miserable, I felt it was better to keep quiet about it for as long as possible. It hasn't been easy, I can tell you. We've had to stretch our imaginations to the limit, working out places to meet where we weren't likely to be seen!'

'Are you in love with him?' Sophie asked.

Tara's face lit up and went bright pink and she nodded.

'How does he feel about you?'

'I think you'd better ask him that,' Tara suggested.

'Well . . . ' Sophie held out her hands and smiled. 'What can I say?'

'How about how happy you are for me?'

'I'm happy for you. In fact I'm extremely happy. I'm still a little bit hurt about the fact you felt you couldn't trust me, but I can't think of anyone I'd rather my brother went out with.' She gave Tara's ankle a little prod with her toe. 'It's OK,' she said, 'I'm starting to forgive you. It might be a slow process, though.'

'Would it help if I gave you a loan of my latest tapes and this month's copy of *Just Seventeen*?' asked Tara, hopefully.

'It might,' replied Sophie, swinging round on her bed so that her back was propped against the wall and her legs were stretched out in front of her. A breeze suddenly blew in through the open window and sent the curtain flapping against a tall, narrow glass vase containing a rose Sophie had picked from the garden. She lurched to grab it before it was knocked over, but a few drops of water had been spilled and she grabbed a tissue and started mopping them up.

When she'd finished, she turned back to Tara. 'Let's have a few more details,' she insisted. 'How did he ask you out? Where did it happen? What happened to Carol-Ann?'

Tara settled herself on the bed next to Sophie and helped herself to a chocolate mint from a packet in the bedside table. 'Mmm — yummy!' she said.

'Do you mean the chocolate or my brother?' asked Sophie, with a snort of laughter.

'Both!' Tara instantly replied. 'OK, so you want the low-down . . . Well, it happened three weeks ago last Thursday at approximately four-twenty-five in the afternoon.'

'Where was I?' asked Sophie. 'Why didn't I see what was going on?'

'You were out. I know because I'd called round to see if you fancied a game of tennis in the park. As you weren't there, and as I had my racquet with me, your

174

thoughtful brother kindly offered to give me a game.'

'Would his offer have had anything remotely to do with the fact that you were wearing the tiniest white shorts in the universe and a top that looked like half a bikini?' enquired Sophie with one eyebrow quizzically raised. She'd seen Tara's tennis outfit before.

'Oh, very probably!' responded Tara airily. Then she gave a broad grin. 'It's the only time I've ever been glad you were out. Just think, if you hadn't been wherever you were — '

'The dentist's, I've just remembered. The filling that never was, because he'd had the x-ray results back and decided he didn't have to do it after all. What a relief!' said Sophie.

'When you've finished your boring babble about the dentist's, I'll continue. That's if you want to hear it . . . ?'

'Of course I do!' Sophie quickly assured her.

'OK. So off we went to the park and found a free tennis court and played a game.'

'Who won?'

'I did,' Tara said proudly.

Richard was a very good tennis player. Sophie wondered if he had gallantly let her win, or if it had been a genuine victory. She hoped it was the latter!

'Then he took me to that café in the park and we had a toasted sandwich and a coffee, except that I couldn't eat my sandwich and your pig-like brother ate two.'

'Typical!' Sophie commented. 'He's always been a greedy-guts.'

'Anyway,' Tara continued, 'the reason I couldn't eat mine was because I was so knocked out by being alone with him. It was what I'd dreamed about for months. He said it was a pity the afternoon had to end and asked me if I'd like to go out with him that evening. We went bowling and then we had a burger and then . . . you won't believe this!'

Tara waited for a reaction but Sophie said nothing, just raised her eyebrows till they vanished into her hair.

'We both thought it was too dangerous to come back together in case anyone saw us so we got almost all the way back and then we stopped by that wall in Hayle Way — 'the snogging wall', Richard's christened it! — and . . . '

'Snogged, by any chance?' asked Sophie.

'By a strange coincidence, yes!' replied Tara.

Sophie sighed wistfully. If only her relationship with Adrian could have happened like that. At the thought of Adrian, her mind clenched like a fist: that beast! that horrible, heartless pig! Her hurt, slighted thoughts must have shown on her face because Tara asked her if she was OK.

'Yes, I'm all right,' she answered resignedly. 'I was just thinking about your brother.'

'Which one?' Tara enquired brightly. 'At least you've only got one.'

'Yes, you've got double the trouble, haven't you?' Sophie commented grimly. She meant it. Boys *were* trouble, whether they were brothers or not! 'In answer to your question, it was Adrian I was thinking about — though I think I'll go back to calling him Ade. I've decided he *is* more of an Ade than an Adrian. Adrian's too poetic for him.'

'And talking of poetic . . . I haven't seen you talking to Mr Poet Laureate-to-be recently. Are you avoiding each other?' asked Tara.

This was such a loaded issue that Sophie didn't quite know what to say. She assumed Ian hadn't mentioned anything to Tara. It was unlikely, because he was such a private person, definitely not a gossip.

'You don't know anything about a . . . a certain poem, do you?'

Tara shook her head. 'What poem?'

'Has he ever shown you his notebook?' Sophie asked.

'No. He guards it with his life,' Tara replied, 'but he does copy the occasional one out and I've seen the things he's had published in the school magazine.'

Sophie fished inside the drawer in her bedside table and withdrew the actual torn-out page from Ian's book. She held it out to Tara, saying, 'Here, you'd better read this, it explains a lot.'

To the accompaniment of several 'wow's and 'I don't believe it's, Tara read it to the end, then handed it back with an admiring look. 'What have you got that I haven't?' she asked. 'Nobody's ever written *me* a poem!'

'I don't think poetry is Richard's strong point. Or music. Remember when he took up the violin?'

Both girls burst into laughter remembering the ghastly scraping and squeaking sounds that used to emanate from Richard's ill-wielded bow.

Tara handed the poem back, saying, 'Well, this *is* a turn-up for the books! What are you going to do?'

'I think you'd better ask Ian that,' said Sophie. She swung herself off the bed and walked over to the window. She pushed the curtain aside and stared moodily out. It was raining and the garden looked dismal and grey, which was just the way she felt. 'He's got it into his head that I'll never get over Ade and that another Cassell is the very last thing on my romantic menu.'

'The fact is, Tara — ' She swung round to face her friend, a distraught, pleading look on her face — 'how can I suddenly switch my affections from one of your brothers to the other? But it's happened. I feel completely dead towards Adrian — oops, *Ade!* — now and I feel an awful lot for Ian. I feel that Ian and I are real soul-mates. But if I started going out with him, what would everyone think? Ade? Your parents? Richard?'

'What do you mean, what would they think?' Tara said. 'They wouldn't think anything. Ade couldn't care less because he's out with Mika every night, I don't think my parents even registered the fact that you were going out with Ade — it wasn't for very long, after all — and as for Richard, I think he'd quite like the idea. In fact, I think he's hoping it will happen.'

'What am I hoping will happen?' said Richard, sticking his head round the door. 'Hi, Tara, I thought I heard your voice.'

'You'd better come in,' Sophie said. 'I'm afraid your secret is out.'

'Oh, Lord,' said Richard, glancing at Tara.

'It's OK,' Sophie said. 'I think it's great.' She hugged her brother. 'Can I be bridesmaid?' she teased.

'Maybe in fifty million years,' Tara replied.

'Seriously though, I thoroughly approve,' Sophie assured them. 'Just be good to each other . . . and don't worry about me, pining away in my ivory tower, a lonely damsel rejected by the world.' She pretended to dash a tear from her eye.

Tara gave a snort. 'You? Lonely? Pull the other one! You've got loads of friends and you know very well that there's one boy who's really, really interested in you. If anyone's pining in their ivory tower right now, it's Ian. Don't think for a minute that he's given up on you. If he heard just one word from you, he might stop using up every scrap of paper in the house practising for his future career as a professional poet.'

Sophie got that warm, funny feeling inside again, thinking of Ian spending so much time and energy thinking about her. She envisaged him on the other side of the wall, so near and yet so far, directing thought-waves at her. She almost felt that she'd picked some of them up. Feelings of longing . . . feelings of love. Oh, he was so lovely. If only there was some way of healing the rift, of letting him know that she *did* care about him.

Richard had a bright idea. 'We could invite him to come out on a foursome with us. Do you think it would work?'

'No,' said Sophie at once. 'It would look like a set-up. It doesn't feel right. No,' she sighed, 'I've got into this and I've got to sort it out somehow. Thank heavens *we're* still friends, Tara!'

'Well, if there's ever anything I can do,

or Richard can do, like talking to Ian — or Ade — on your behalf,' Tara said.

'Thanks for offering, but no thanks,' Sophie replied. 'This is my mess and I've got to sort it out. Ian decided it was best to keep a low profile for a while, till everything was over and forgotten, and I think he was right.'

'Well, don't sit in your room and mope. The rain's stopped, it's clearing up. Why don't we all go to the park?' suggested Richard.

'I don't want to play gooseberry,' said Sophie.

Tara tweaked her arm. 'Of course you're not playing gooseberry! We can't kiss and walk at the same time, so you're not spoiling anything. Come on!'

'OK,' Sophie agreed, shoving her feet into her trainers.

★   ★   ★

Why is it that fate always decides to play tricks on you when you least expect it? When you're all geared up for something to happen, it never does. And then, when you're happily going about your daily activities, not particularly wishing or pining for anything, suddenly *shazam!* Some mischievous genie appears out of nowhere and creates havoc in your life.

Just as Sophie was leaving the house, chattering happily with Tara and Richard, the door of number twenty-two was flung open and two figures came bounding noisily out. One had four legs. It was a big-footed, floppy-eared, fat, brown-and-white puppy which looked as if it had some beagle blood in it. The other had two legs and was grinning merrily as he hauled on the lead.

'Hi, Ian,' said Tara. 'Are you taking Beanbag to the park? That's where we're going. Come and join us.'

18

'Who does Beanbag belong to?' asked Sophie.

'Why didn't you tell me about him?' Honestly, she thought huffily, she seemed to get left out of everything these days!

'I never thought about it. You see, he's not ours, we're only borrowing him,' Tara replied. She reached down and fondled the animal's silky ears. It bounced up and licked her hand. 'He belongs to Uncle Jimmy and Auntie Mary. They got him a month ago but they've gone away for a few days and couldn't take him with them — '

' — so we offered to look after him to save him having to go into the kennels,' interrupted Ian, finishing the story.

'Why's he called Beanbag?' asked Sophie curiously.

'He's fat and full of beans, as you can see. That's one reason — ' began Tara.

' — and the other is that when Auntie Mary and Uncle Jimmy first brought him to visit us, he ate a big beanbag cushion that Ade had on his bedroom floor. He went into total destruct mode, tore it to shreds. There were beans everywhere and we had to stop him eating them before he got sick,' finished Ian.

'He's great. He's just utterly lovable. I wish he was ours,' Ian said. He looked from the puppy to Sophie, his eyes glowing with the affection he felt for the animal. For her, too? How could Sophie tell? That look was mesmerizing her.

She felt quivery inside and tore her eyes away from his gaze, directing her attention to the lolloping puppy. 'Can I hold him?' she asked.

'He's stronger than you think,' said Ian. 'You'll have to keep a tight hold of the lead and not let him get away. He has to be kept on the lead all the time. He hasn't learnt any road sense yet. He's just about to start puppy training classes.'

Ian transferred the lead to Sophie's hand. As she took the handle, he kept his hand clasped over hers. Her hand fluttered in his grasp like a frightened bird, then relaxed.

'That's right,' he said. 'Just keep hold. Don't let the lead out any more. Keep him under control.'

He took his hand off Sophie's and she

was amazed at how disappointed she felt. He was treating her exactly the same as he'd done prior to giving her the poem — as an old friend and neighbour. Nothing special. Yet she knew she *was* special to him — and he to her. How could she ever let him know? It seemed impossible. If only she could write poems and put one through his door . . . But she knew she couldn't.

Maybe I could copy out some lines from *Romeo and Juliet*, she thought. But that wasn't the same as writing something herself.

She was soon absorbed in controlling the scampering pup, which seemed to take an interest in everything. He would stop to sniff something and she would nearly trip over him. Then he would bounce off to the right, to the left, tangling the lead round everyone. He was annoying, he was fun, he was adorable.

When they got to the park, Ian produced a much-chewed rubber ball from his pocket. 'Throw the ball and play out as much lead as you can,' he said. 'Beanbag will bring it back to you.'

She obeyed, hurling the battered ball. It had hardly left her hand before Beanbag was off. Sophie pressed the button to release more lead. It was a bit like flying a kite. Beanbag pounced on the ball, growling and worrying it, then gambolled back and deposited the spitty article at her feet. His wet, pink tongue hung out and he cocked his head comically, asking her to throw it again.

'Ugh! I'm not picking up *that*!' Sophie exclaimed.

So Ian gave the ball a swipe with his foot which sent it rocketing into the shrubbery. This time they had to restrain the panting, yapping dog before the lead did too much damage to the bushes.

Their games with Beanbag had taken them away from the spot where Richard and Tara were standing talking. Simultaneously, she and Ian halted and looked at each other.

'I — '

'Isn't it — '

They had both started talking at once and now they burst out laughing. Sophie suddenly felt gloriously elated. The day seemed brighter, the grass seemed greener — everything seemed more vivid and alive.

'I'm glad we've bumped into one

another. Sorry I've been avoiding you,' said Ian.

'That makes two of us,' confessed Sophie. Her heart was thudding. She knelt down to stroke Beanbag. When she looked up at Ian, she was amazed to see the sun lighting his hair to a blazing chestnut shade. It looked incredible. Just add a cloak and he would look like a true lord of Framlingham Castle. What on earth could have made her think it was Ade? She imagined Ian hurling the usurper off the castle battlements, then shook her head to clear the image. She didn't hate Ade so much that she wished him dead. She didn't hate anyone right now, not with this fizzy, bubbly feeling inside her, like champagne in her veins.

She stood up again. 'I wish I could tell you how much I admire you,' she said.

Ian inclined his head and gave her a quizzical look. 'Then tell me,' he said. His voice was low, intense, slightly husky as if he, like her, was suddenly finding it difficult to breathe.

'Ian Cassell, I admire you for being honest and sincere and kind and a brilliant poet, and for being braver than anyone I know about coming out with

188

your true feelings.'

He looked down and away, then back to her again. 'What else could I do? You were worth taking a risk for.'

She wanted to ask, 'Am I still?' but she couldn't get the words out. She lacked Ian's courage. But there was one more thing she just had to tell him. 'It's more than just 'admire',' she said.

Beanbag started whining for attention but Sophie ignored him. She had to. It was one of those moments where nothing mattered but the feelings that were zapping between them in the wordless silence.

A silence which Ian broke with a, 'Look!'

He pointed to a tree where two squirrels were following each other up and down and all around the trunk, in a comical chase. Sophie laughed and clutched at his arm. He jumped and she withdrew her fingers and found them tingling where they had made contact with his body. Had she been too forward? Maybe she shouldn't have touched him. Perhaps it was too soon.

She looked at him. He had his back to the sun and his high-cheek-boned face was in shadow while she squinted against the glaring light. She wished she'd brought her sun-glasses, to protect herself both from the sunlight, and from Ian's penetrating gaze. She was zinging inside from all kinds of mixed-up feelings. Excitement, apprehension, wonderment, and something else too important to name. Something so strong that it completely blotted out the imagined emotions she'd felt for Ade.

'Sophie . . . ' He spoke her name so low that she sensed rather than heard it.

Something was pulling them towards each other. The sun was no longer in her eyes for Ian's face was there in front of hers, so close . . . And now his lips were hovering, just about to touch hers, just brushing hers and she was dying, collapsing, melting, flying into a million pieces as he kissed her.

'Oh, Ian!' she whispered rapturously, clinging to him for support, squeezing him so hard it was a wonder his ribs didn't break. 'Oh, Ian . . . ' she repeated.

It was all she could say but it meant a million things. So much was whizzing through her head. Memories . . . Ian and herself by the river when she was eleven, while he patiently instructed her on how to fish; the day she and Ian had got lost in a wood during a Cassell-Thompson family picnic and he had stopped her crying and panicking and helped them both find their way back; Ian falling off a donkey on the beach at Broadstairs when its saddle slid under its belly; Ian in the sea, teaching herself and Tara to do the crawl until some seaweed got tangled round his ankle and he thought it was a jellyfish and yelled and they all laughed.

Happy days, happy memories — and Ian was a part of them all. A part of her childhood, a part of her growing-up process. Almost a part of her. He was so very, very precious. And so clever, kind, sensitive, funny . . . How could she ever have let herself be distracted by Ade? Thinking about it now, Sophie felt that she had always loved Ian. It had just taken until now to realize it.

She remembered a passage from the Bible that they'd studied in school: *To everything there is a season.* Maybe this was her season for falling in love with Ian!

His arm was around her, pulling her close to him again. Beanbag for once was silent, spread out on the grass and dozing. The last thing Sophie was aware of before being lost in the best, most passionate kiss she had ever received, was the sound of a blackbird's sweet, piercing song. It seemed to contain all the beauty and promise of a long, perfect summer of love.

THE END

We do hope that you have enjoyed reading this large print book.

Did you know that all of our titles are available for purchase?

We publish a wide range of high quality large print books including:
Romances, Mysteries, Classics, General Fiction, Non Fiction and Westerns.

Special interest titles available in large print are:
The Little Oxford Dictionary Music Book, Song Book Hymn Book, Service Book

Also available from us courtesy of Oxford University Press:
Young Readers' Dictionary (large print edition) Young Readers' Thesaurus (large print edition)

For further information or a free brochure, please contact us at:
Ulverscroft Large Print Books Ltd., The Green, Bradgate Road, Anstey, Leicester, LE7 7FU, England. Tel: (00 44) **0116 236 4325 Fax:** (00 44) **0116 234 0205**

Other titles in the
Spectrum Imprint:

EVE'S PARTY

Nick Turnbull

Normally the old folk of Portlecombe
love to spin a yarn. But mention 1936,
and everyone clams up. Something bad
happened back then. Something connected to the weird events of the last
few days . . . Killer sharks in the bay.
Dogs turned savage. Strange laughter
in the hills . . . And Eve. Quiet, smiling,
red-headed Eve. She's having a party.
It's a kind of reunion. For anyone who
survived her last one . . . Some stories
are best left — buried.